To Michelle,

Nice to have met you @ the lunch table today. God bless in all you do.

Love,

Jim Tona

A Gil Leduc Mystery

The Purity Ring Murders

Jim Toner

Bloomington, IN

Milton Keynes, UK

AuthorHouse™
1663 Liberty Drive, Suite 200
Bloomington, IN 47403
www.authorhouse.com
Phone: 1-800-839-8640

AuthorHouse™ UK Ltd.
500 Avebury Boulevard
Central Milton Keynes, MK9 2BE
www.authorhouse.co.uk
Phone: 08001974150

First published by AuthorHouse 6/13/2006
Printed in the United States of America
Bloomington, Indiana

ISBN: 1-4259-2841-2 (sc)
ISBN: 1-4259-2842-0 (dj)

This book is printed on acid-free paper.

Library of Congress Control Number: 2006902821

Prologue

Three years earlier in Tours, France

Thirteen year-old Gil Leduc paced around his uncle's living room. In a few minutes he would accompany his uncle and his cousin Angéline to the train station in Tours, France where he was spending the summer.

Angéline grabbed the tail of his navy blue t-shirt. "Sit down. You're making me nervous."

Gil waved his arms. "You know I can't wait to see Marie."

He was referring to Marie Chauvet, Angéline's friend, who he had met at summer camp. Like Angéline, she was fifteen years old.

At the camp Gil had spent much time with her. A week later he and Angéline, had visited her in Blois where her parents owned a few hotels. The three teens swam under the moonlit sky one night at the Novotel.

That night Marie showed Gil her purity ring. She and Angéline had promised both God and one another that they would abstain from sex until marriage.

"Promise me one thing, Gil, " said Marie.

"What's that?"

"You'll do the same."

"I will."

Marie promptly threw her arms around him. She was the first girl who had ever hugged him.

Gil's Uncle Claude entered the living room. "Let's go, kids. By the time we get there, the train should have arrived from Blois."

About five minutes later they arrived at the train station. A crowd of people gathered in a circle near the tracks. *What's going on,* wondered Gil.

As they approached the tracks, a guy in his twenties with dark, curly hair passed them going in the opposite direction. Gil knew he had seen him somewhere before. But where, he thought.

A couple of uniformed officers pushed through the crowd. Uncle Claude, who was the chief inspector of the police in Tours, raced in the station and pushed through the crowd identifying himself as a police officer. His face was expressionless.

Gil, who wanted to follow in his uncle and grandfather's footsteps, followed his uncle. He stood in horror as he watched the police break through the circle. *Marie Chauvet lay on the ground. Her yellow t-shirt was soaked with blood.* Her outstretched hand contained the purity ring.

Gil buried his face in his hands. He couldn't understand who would want to kill a fun-loving girl like Marie. Angéline led him to a bench. The cousins hugged each other. Tears streamed down their cheeks.

Chapter One

Three years later-Toronto, Ontario

Gil woke up out of a deep sleep. He once again had the reoccurring nightmare about Marie. His heart raced. As he rose up in bed, he shouted, "Marie!"

"Gil, get up!" shouted his girlfriend Jan Barrio as she swung a pillow at him conking him in the head. "We're going to be late."

Gil opened his eyes. Behind his girlfriend stood Jan's father Pablo Barrio. The Niagara Falls police officer shook his head. "I don't know, Gil. I think you're in hot soup."

Gil slowly rose out of bed. He and Jan were to meet Jan's friend April Ames that morning for breakfast. Gil, however, had slept in. He was in Toronto for a brief vacation with the Barrios. Mr. Barrio was attending a conference at Police Headquarters.

"Well, get up," yelled Jan. "It's not like you to be late."

Gil took a quick shower and put on a navy blue t-shirt and black jeans. As he grabbed his jean jacket, Jan grabbed him by the hand pulling him out the door of his hotel room.

Mr. Barrio could only stand there smiling.

Jan, a tall, slender girl with dyed blond hair, wore jeans and a t-shirt and cap of the San Jose Giants, the team her father had pitched for. She held Gil's hand as they walked toward the subway station. "So, who's this Marie? You better not be looking at any other girls."

Gil, who at six foot four, had about a half a foot on Jan. "A girl I'd met when I returned to France three years ago."

"How come you never mentioned her?"

Gil stared at the ground. Even three years later it was still difficult for him to discuss it. "She was murdered."

Jan gasped. She grabbed Gil's elbow. "I'm so sorry. Will you forgive me?"

Gil wrapped her in his arms. "Of course."

In the subway car, Jan asked him, "What was this girl like?"

"A true Christian. Fun-loving. She was a model."

"Oh, wow. Just like April."

Jan brushed back her ponytail. "Was her murder ever solved?"

Gil shook his head.

About twenty minutes later Gil and Jan arrived at the North York Centre. They had planned to meet April at Café Balzac. Gil's stomach growled. He couldn't wait to taste the hot chocolate and croissants.

Gil checked his watch. "We're late. I hope April won't be upset."

Jan nudged Gil. "Don't worry. April's not like that. I was only worried you wouldn't get up this morning."

Gil was about to say something when he heard a girl scream. "Oh, no. It's April."

Jan grabbed his jacket sleeve. "Let's go."

The two teenagers ran upstairs toward the library, where they spotted the tall, blond April by the bulletin board hanging up a poster.

April screamed, "Don't shoot me."

Gil grabbed his cell phone and promptly dialed 9-1-1. A person dressed like a Shiite Muslim pointed a revolver at April.

Jan shouted, "Don't shoot my friend."

The person pointed the gun right at Jan and fired at her. Gil promptly tackled Jan; the bullet just missed his head. The person shot April twice in the chest.

Gil watched in horror as he reached for his cell phone.

A dispatcher said, "Hello. Is somebody there?"

Gil's heart raced. "Shots fired at the North York Centre library. Girl down."

Once the Shiite darted out of the building, Jan raced over to her wounded friend.

The dispatcher asked, "May I have your name please?"

"Gil Leduc."

"Your phone number, Mr. Leduc?"

"347-2665."

"We have a police cruiser and ambulance on the way."

Jan, who was leaning over her wounded friend, cried, "Gil, give me your jacket."

Gil handed her his jacket, which she pressed against April's wounded chest.

Sweat poured down Jan's face as she tried to save her friend. "April, it's Jan.

Who did this to you?"

April muttered something.

"April, I couldn't hear you."

April's head, however, dropped to the side.

Jan shook her friend. "April, don't die on me."

Gil knelt by April and checked for a pulse. Tears formed in his eyes, as he found none.

He shook his head. "She's dead."

Jan held up April's left hand on which she wore her purity ring. "April, I'll keep the promise I made to you."

Last year the girls attended a Christian concert after which they obtained the rings and promised each other to abstain from sex until marriage.

Tears streamed down Jan's cheeks. "She was one of my better friends."

Gil wrapped his arms around her and pressed his lips against her cheek. "I'm sorry."

A crowd of people gathered around them. Two of the centre's security guards urged people to back away from the body. Gil and Jan sat at a table near April as they waited

for the police to arrive. Jan grabbed Gil's hand. "We need to find out who did this to April."

Gil shook his head. "I promised my mom I wouldn't get involved so soon in another mystery."

Gil and Jan both hoped to become police officers. They had helped the police solve a few mysteries.

Jan punched his upper arm. "Come on, Gil. A mama's boy, you're not."

Gil stood up when he saw a short, stocky constable approach the scene. The constable approached the body. His nametag read Barry S. Olsen. "Are you the one who called this in?"

Gil nodded. He tried to speak, but couldn't. He had to look away from April's body.

His heart raced as he saw a man leave the library. *It was the same man he had seen three years earlier in Tours.*

"Your name?" asked Sloan.

Gil managed to tell him. He wiped away tears with a handkerchief.

"Your address?"

"1845 Benjamin Drive."

Sloan looked blank. "I take it you're not from Toronto."

"No. Niagara Falls, New York."

"You know this girl?"

Gil stared at the ground. "Her name's April Ames."

More police officers arrived at the scene. One of them cordoned off the area with the yellow ribbon stating "Crime Scene-Don't Pass."

Sloan placed the end of his pen in his mouth. "What brings you to Toronto?"

Gil ran his fingers through his dark, curly hair. "My girlfriend and I hoped to spend time with April. Now, we... can't."

Sloan patted Gil's shoulder. "I'm sorry."

At that moment a tall, lanky man dressed in blue jeans, a striped t-shirt and a black leather jacket approached the scene. His detective shield was clipped to his belt. "What have we got here, Sloan?"

The constable pointed to April's dead body. "Someone shot this girl, Hilger."

Sloan introduced Gil to Detective Constable Adam Hilger. Gil told Hilger what he had just told Sloan.

Hilger brought out a pen and notebook from his jacket pocket. "Let's sit down over there."

Gil followed the detective to a bench across from the library.

Hilger asked, "How do you know this girl?"

Gil once again wiped away tears. "She's a friend of my girlfriend. We met her last year at a concert."

"You had planned to meet her this morning?"

Gil nodded. "Now our plans are ruined."

Hilger patted Gil's back. "I'm sorry. When was the last time you saw her?"

"About three weeks ago on Memorial Day weekend."

"Had she been in any trouble?"

Gil felt a lump in his throat. "Yes."

"What do you mean?"

"She was thinking of leaving the modeling industry. It was too competitive for her.

My girlfriend would know more."

Jan hung her head as she approached them. "I never thought this would happen to her."

Hilger pointed his pen at her. "Is she your girlfriend, Gil?"

"Yes."

"Your name, young lady?"

"Jan Barrio."

"I'm sorry about your friend. Please answer my questions the best you can. Where do you live?"

"789 76th Street."

"Also in Niagara Falls, New York?"

"Yes."

Hilger squeezed her hand. "When did you last see her?"

"Memorial Day weekend. We had such a good time together. Now she's gone."

Jan burst into tears. Gil wrapped his arms around her and rubbed her back.

Hilger patted her shoulder. "I realize this is a rough time for you, but what can you tell me about your friend?"

"She was a model with the Francisco Modeling Agency. Last week she spent a few days in Orillia on a model shoot. She didn't want to model anymore."

"Would you know why?"

"She wanted to tell me today. Now, she can't."

More tears streamed down Jan's cheeks. Gil wiped away her tears.

Hilger said, "I know it's hard right now, but is there anything else you can tell me?"

Jan pointed her index finger toward the ceiling. "Wait! I got something."

"What's that?" asked Gil.

"I also saw her on Victoria Day weekend. She had a modeling shoot at Port Dalhousie.

We were at the beach when one of our teachers approached us."

"Who?"

"Bartholomew"

Hilger touched Jan's arm. "What happened?"

"I introduced April to him. She seemed very nervous the whole time."

"Why?"

"He made suggestive comments about her."

"What a pig!" exclaimed Gil. "I can't believe it."

Hilger asked, "Do you think this might have to do with the murder?"

Chapter Two

Jan shrugged. "I don't know. But I don't trust Bartholomew. I just know he didn't kill her."

Hilger pinched his chin. "How do you know?"

Gil said, " Whoever shot her was tall, thin and dressed in Shiite Muslim garb. Bartholomew is about five foot eight and husky."

"Tell me more about Bartholomew."

Gil adjusted his shirt. "His name is Peter J. Bartholomew. He teaches English at Niagara East High. He lives in St. Catharines."

Hilger tapped Jan with his pen. "What else don't you like about this Bartholomew?"

"He holds wild parties at his house with underage girls. He invited April and me to his house. We refused."

Hilger bit his lower lip. "You did the right thing. Never go over anyone's house if you have any suspicions at all."

After a lull in the conversation Hilger asked, "Did April have any problems with any Arabs?"

Jan shook her head. "No. I doubt she even knew any Shiite Muslims."

"Where did April live?"

"On Park Home Avenue with her mom."

"Anything else?"

Gil hung his head. "No, but we intend to find out."

Hilger held up his hand. "Wait. You're only kids. Leave this to the police. Here's my card in case you think of anything else." The detective paused a moment. "What kind of a person was April?"

Jan replied, " A good Christian girl who wouldn't hurt a fly. She was very shy."

"But she was a model?

"A family counselor suggested she try it."

Hilger shook his head. "It's a dangerous profession. Possibly more dangerous than being a cop. I've seen so many of these girls end up dead." Hilger adjusted his glasses.

"Others end up becoming prostitutes."

Jan wrinkled her face. "That's disgusting. April would never have done that. She vowed not to have sex until she married."

"Did she have any other enemies besides Bartholomew?"

Jan frowned. "None that I know of. I just know it was hard for her to make friends with the other models. She was not a competitive person like so many of the other models."

"Any family?"

"Only her mom. Her father ran off when she was just a little girl. The poor girl had had

so many problems in her life."

More tears ran down Jan's cheeks. Gil wrapped his arm around her.

Jan said, "Sorry we can't be of more help."

Hilger smiled. "No, you've been very helpful. Call me if you can think of anything else."

"We will," said Gil.

Half an hour later Gil and Jan arrived at Francisco Modeling Agency. A receptionist pointed to the waiting room. The teens hoped to talk to Marsha Tulino, April's agent. About five minutes later a short, dark-haired woman around thirty years old entered the room. She wore a tan business suit. On looking in their direction, her face broke into a wide grin. She extended her hand to Jan. "Nice to see you again."

Jan accepted the extended hand. "Same here. This is my boyfriend, Gil Leduc."

The woman extended her hand to Gil. "Nice to meet you. I'm Marsha Tulino. April told me you've solved a few mysteries."

Gil shook her hand. "Nice to meet you, Ms. Tulino."

"Please call me, Marsha. What brings you here? The two of you seem sad." Marsha glanced at her watch. "Come to think about it. Where's April? It's not like her to be late."

Jan stared at the floor. "That's why we're here."

Marsha stood stunned. "You mean something's happened to her?"

Gil touched her elbow. He felt a lump in his throat. "We... better...talk somewhere else. "

"We can talk in my office. Why don't the two of you follow me?"

Without hesitation they followed her to her office. They sat on chairs in front of her desk. Pictures of many beautiful girls hung on the wall behind her chair.

"What happened to April?"

Jan told her.

Marsha's eyes widened. "Oh, no. She was one of my favorite girls."

Tears formed in Jan's eyes. "She always spoke well of you. You were like the sister she never had."

Marsha wiped away tears. "Yes, she told me."

Gil asked, " I know this may not be the time to ask, but when was the last time you saw her?"

"Yesterday."

"What kind of a mood was she in?"

"She seemed worried."

"In what way?"

"April was right. You sure are inquisitive."

Jan patted Gil's arm. "Honey, please."

Gil shook his head. "I'm sorry, mam. I realize this is a shock to you. We can return later."

Marsha blew her nose. "It's okay. She'd had a bad experience last week in Orillia."

"What happened?"

"A photographer was dealing drugs at the motel."

Jan exclaimed, "Oh, no. April was totally against drugs."

"So, am I."

Gil rubbed his chin as he thought what he would ask Marsha next." What was April worried about?"

Marsha twirled her black hair. "She and I had planned to go to the police today."

"But why here in Toronto when she was in Orillia?"

"The man she suspects has also been suspected of drug dealing here in our city."

Gil adjusted his glasses. "That's terrible. We heard she wanted to quit modeling."

"Yes, the poor thing was so despondent yesterday. She was one of my favorites.

I hate to lose her."

"So, do we. She was a nice girl."

"Also this is a tough business. She always told me how the Lord had brought her through times. I became a Christian through her."

Gil smiled at Jan. "That's great."

Jan said, "That would be April. She really lived what she believed."

Marsha said, "That's unfortunately why many of the other girls didn't like her.

They mocked her for her beliefs."

Gil shook his head. "I couldn't find a reason to not like her."

Tears trickled down Marsha's cheeks. "I know what you mean. I loved her."

Jan hugged Marsha. "I loved her too."

Marsha's phone rang. She answered it. "Sorry to cut this short. I have to meet someone in the food court."

"May we talk later?"

Marsha handed him a business card. "Sure. Call first though. This agency is as busy as a beehive."

Gil and Jan left the agency. They headed to the food court after briefly visiting a couple of stores. Gil touched Jan's arm.

"I wish we could have asked her more."

Jan said, "I know what you mean."

A police officer raced toward the food court. Gil pointed to him. "I wonder what's going on."

Gil and Jan followed the officer to the food court. A crowd of people gathered around the women's washroom. The officer ordered the people to stand back.

Gil caught a glimpse of the body. "Oh, no! It's Marsha!"

Chapter Three

The constable frowned. "You knew her?"

"Just met her a few minutes ago."

The tall, broad shouldered officer's face tightened. "Would you have a reason to kill her?"

Gil froze stunned by the question. How could the officer so quickly accuse him of murder?

"Well?" asked the officer.

"No," mumbled Gil.

"Speak up."

Jan stepped forward. "Excuse me, officer. I knew this woman. She was a friend of one of my friends."

The officer took their names and addresses. At that moment a tall, dark-haired man dressed in a dark, navy suit approached them. "Problem here, Wathan?"

Wathan pointed to Gil and Jan. "These kids know the deceased."

The dark-haired man introduced himself as Detective Sergeant William O'Donnell.

On hearing the information from Wathan, O'Donnell asked, "You're not runaways, are you?"

Gil's face tightened. He couldn't believe the detective's question. "No."

Jan pleaded. "Officer, please. A close friend of ours was murdered this morning.

Now this woman ends up dead. You have…"

O'Donnell pointed his pen at Jan. "Answer my question."

Jan said, "We're here on vacation with my parents. My dad's attending a conference at Police Headquarters."

O'Donnell pointed to Gil. "Where are your parents, young man?"

"Marseille, France."

"Doing what?"

"Teaching English."

Gil's parents were both French teachers. They were spending the summer with his aunt and her family.

O'Donnell scratched his eyebrow. "Back to my question. Would either of you have a reason to kill this woman?"

Before Gil could say anything, Hilger ran to the scene. "Bill, please. Ease up on these kids."

O'Donnell straightened. "Adam, I'm your senior officer."

"I know. How can you accuse these kids of anything? I saw them earlier this morning."

O'Donnell frowned. "That's enough. Take these kids away."

Gil shook his head. *O'Donnell must hate kids, he thought.*

Hilger led Gil and Jan to a table in the food court. "Don't take it personally. He's the father of a few teenagers. All he ever does is complain about his kids."

Jan explained to Hilger about their meeting with Marsha.

Hilger tapped the table with his pen. "Sounds like someone had found out about their plan."

Gil frowned. "I know. But who?"

Jan placed her head on the table. "Someone must have overheard their conversation. They might have been in Marsha's office, and someone must have been eavesdropping."

Gil wrinkled his forehead. "Even had the door been closed, someone still could have overheard."

Hilger said, "I'll find out who was at the agency yesterday."

Jan held up her hand. "Wait. There's something I need to tell you."

Hilger pointed his pen at her. "What?"

"My mom has a friend who works at the agency."

"Really? What's her name?"

"Ramona Gonzales. She's an old college friend of my mom. I know my mom's tried to contact her. We were hoping to see her this weekend."

"No luck so far?"

Jan shook her head. "No."

Hilger folded his hands. "Like I said. Call me the moment you find out anything."

"We will."

A few minutes later Gil and Jan descended the staircase to the subway station. When they got to the platform, someone tapped Gil on the shoulder. His heart raced. Who would he know he was here?

"Out to solve another case?" asked the voice behind him.

Gil didn't recognize the voice. After all, he didn't know anybody with an English accent. He pivoted on one foot. Just who was this person?

Chapter Four

On seeing his English teacher, Gil breathed a deep sigh of relief. "Oh, Mr. Bartholomew. I should have realized it was you."

Mr. Bartholomew, a stocky gray-haired man, extended his hand to Gil, who shook it firmly. Jan did likewise. Bartholomew loved drama and often imitated actors.

The teacher asked, "What brings you here?"

Gil replied, "A mini-vacation with Jan and family. What about you?"

"I come here often. I like plays, especially Shakespearean ones."

Gil was curious as to why Bartholomew would be at that particular subway stop.

Maybe he was visiting the Metro Library. At this time, however, he didn't want to ask the teacher any more questions. After all, he didn't want to let Bartholomew know he suspected he had a part in the murders.

The subway train halted. Gil and Jan hopped in. Before the door shut, Gil glanced back. Bartholomew had boarded the same train.

As they plopped down on their seats, Gil whispered to Jan. "I wonder why he's really here."

Jan shrugged. "Hard to say. The man is dangerous. Rumor has it he dabbles in child pornography."

"Sick!" exclaimed Gil.

Jan pressed her index finger against her lips. "Quiet."

"Sorry."

About half an hour later Gil and Jan arrived at Mrs. Ames's house. A tall, husky blond-haired woman answered the door. Her eyes were red. She wiped away tears with a handkerchief. She wore black pants and a black sports coat. On seeing the youths, she smiled. "I'm so glad you came. Please come in."

Jan wrapped her arm around Mrs. Ames. "I'm so sorry about April. She was one of the better friends I had."

Mrs. Ames patted Jan's arm. "I know she was..." She covered her face with her handkerchief unable to finish to finish her sentence.

After wiping away more tears she extended her hand to Gil. "April spoke well of you too."

Gil held her hand between his. He shook his head. "I wish I were meeting you under different circumstances. We were thankful to have a friend like her."

Mrs. Ames pointed to the living room. "Let's sit in there. I'm sure on a hot day like today, you kids could use a drink." She approached the kitchen.

Jan said, "I'll get it. Go sit down."

A moment later Jan brought back two glasses of root beer. "How was April this morning? "I can't even imagine how this must be for you."

Mrs. Ames said, "I never thought this would happen to her. She was frightened."

"How so?" asked Gil.

Mrs. Ames hesitated a moment. "It was hard for her to talk. It was ...like she knew something would happen."

Jan's jaw dropped. "This is even worse than I thought."

"She and Marsha were supposed to go to the police today concerning a certain photographer."

Jan's eyes widened. "Oh, my. She must have suspected someone found out."

Gil rubbed his chin. "I realize this is a rough time for you, but do you know the photographer's name?"

Mrs. Ames shook her head. "Sorry. I don't. I'm bad with names as it is."

Jan asked, "Other than that, did April say much about her time in Orillia?"

Mrs. Ames rubbed her nose. "She liked the town. She, however, suspected drug dealing." She stared at the floor. A minute later she looked up. "The photographer wanted to take nude pictures of her."

Jan waved her arms. "How gross."

"He wouldn't take no for an answer."

Jan hung her head. "Poor April. What a way to go." She wiped away tears. "She didn't deserve to die like that."

"Brandon and this photographer had had words."

"You mean April's boyfriend?"

"Yes."

Gil glanced out the living room window. Jan nudged him. "What's wrong?"

"A black Grand Am keeps driving by."

Mrs. Ames shook her head. "Don't know anyone who drives a car like that."

Jan reasoned, "Could be someone just looking for an address."

Gil shook his head. "I doubt it."

Jan asked, "Did April have any problems with the models?"

Mrs. Ames blew her nose. "It's a very competitive business. Not too many nice girls are models."

Gil interjected, "But did she have any problems with anyone in particular?"

"Yes. Her name's Naomi. She lives just a couple blocks from here."

Color drained from Jan's face. "Oh, my goodness. That my mom's friend Ramona's daughter."

Gil raised his index finger. "Maybe this isn't the time to ask, but what did this Naomi do to make April's life so miserable?"

Mrs. Ames sipped some water. "She kept calling her a prude and making fun of her stance on sexual purity."

Jan pushed back her hair. "Never thought Naomi would do something like that.

I've known her all my life."

"Some of the other girls didn't like April because she didn't use drugs or drink. They kept telling her that's where the real living was at."

"Well, that's not true."

"I second it," said Gil.

Jan stood up. "Gil, I think we better go. Mrs. Ames, I'll give you my cell phone number. Call me should you think of anything else."

Mrs. Ames wrapped her arms around Jan. "I will. Thanks for coming."

A few minutes later Gil and Jan approached the Gonzales residence, a split-level house. Jan rang the doorbell. After waiting a moment, she rang again. Still nobody answered.

Jan shrugged her shoulders. "I guess nobody's home."

Gil noticed a black car slowing down as they crossed the street. "It's the same car I saw pass by Mrs. Ames's house."

"Maybe they..." Jan never finished her sentence.

Someone jumped out of the car and yelled, "Get the girl."

Chapter Five

Without hesitation Gil and Jan ran as fast as they could. The black sports car tried to cut them off on Mrs. Ames's street, but Gil and Jan dove on the sidewalk just in time. Gil got up. Two husky men raced toward them. Gil and Jan got up and darted toward Yonge Street. The car made a U-turn, but collided with another vehicle.

Once the teens reached Yonge Street, they immediately entered the subway and headed toward College Avenue.

Inside the subway car Gil breathed a deep sigh of relief. "That was too close for comfort."

"Someone must have been praying for us."

"You can say that again."

Gil frowned, however. He didn't understand why someone would have been after Jan. He wrapped his arm around her. "Why would someone be after you?"

"I believe it was from my visit here on Memorial Day weekend."

Gil rubbed his chin. "I know you came home upset about something."

"I never told you the whole thing."

"It's okay. Tell me now."

"The whole time April and I were at the beach a couple of guys kept staring at us. I could overhear them making suggestive comments about us. Later we saw them back in town."

"Then what happened?"

"We were having supper when the same two guys approached us. They hit on us. I told them I was taken, but they didn't stop. So, I threw my coke in the one guy's face."

"Those pigs will pay for this."

Jan tugged at his shirt. "Well, I didn't let them get away with it."

"Then what happened?"

"April poured water down the other guy's shirt. He took a swing at her. That's when the restaurant manager told them to leave. Actually, we, too, got a warning."

"Let's call, Hilger." Gil dialed the detective's number. A moment later the detective answered. Gil told him about the men chasing them.

Gil covered the phone a moment. "Hilger wants to know if April knew the men."

"Give me the phone."

Gil handed it to Jan. How he wanted to rip the men's faces off who were hitting on her.

Jan said, "Adam, April believed she'd seen the men with the photographer at the studio. They were constantly hitting on the models."

"Should you see them again," said Hilger. "Call the police immediately."

"Will do."

About ten minutes later Gil and Jan entered Maple Leaf Gardens hoping to find Brandon. A husky man headed in their direction.

Jan held up her finger. "Excuse me. Do you know Brandon Batista?"

The man frowned. "Sorry. Don't know him."

Gil and Jan approached the hockey rink. Gil asked one of the players if he knew Brandon.

The player replied, "Yes, I know him. He left practice early. He just couldn't concentrate. His girlfriend having died and all."

Jan stared at the ground. "I tried to save her."

The player patted her arm. "I'm sorry."

Gil nodded. "Can't imagine what he'd be going through. Any idea where we might find him?"

The player folded his arms. "You could try the Eaton Centre. He might have gone to Indigo or a sporting goods store."

"Thanks."

About ten minutes later Gil and Jan walked through the first floor of Indigo. Gil reasoned a guy close to his age might want to leaf through a sports magazine or an entertainment magazine. No one resembling an athlete was near the magazine section.

They climbed the stairs to the second floor of the store. Both teens thought Brandon could be in the video section. He might have been looking for a movie to watch.

The section, however, was loaded with little kids wanting their mothers to buy them the latest Walt Disney movie or young teenage boys checking out videos of their favorite rock bands.

They headed to the Starbucks within the store. Jan shook her head. "He's not here either."

Gil and Jan headed to the teen section, but still saw no trace of Brandon.

For an hour Gil and Jan searched for Brandon in numerous stores. Unfortunately they did not find him.

Gil nudged Jan. "I don't know about you, but I'm thirsty."

"I'm with you, buddy."

About five minutes later Gil and Jan entered the mall's north end food court. Sitting at a table was the tall, bespectacled Brandon Batista. His face broke into a wide smile. His eyes were blood shot. "You found me."

Jan had met Brandon during her spring break trip to Toronto. She extended her hand to him. "Sorry about April She was a good friend." After a brief pause Jan pointed to Gil. "This is my boyfriend Gil Leduc."

After Brandon accepted Jan's extended hand, he shook Gil's hand. "Nice to meet you."

"Same here. Just wish we were meeting under different circumstances."

Brandon pointed to the empty chairs in front of him. He was probably around six foot tall and had a slender athletic build. "Sit down."

"Sure." Gil and Jan plopped down in the chairs.

Gil folded his hands. "Sorry about April."

"Thank you." Brandon nodded. "I loved her."

"I'm sure you did. I can't fathom why someone would do this to her."

Brandon wiped away tears. "You thirsty?"

"Yes."

Brandon handed him a ten-dollar bill. "Here. It's on me. I know you guys probably don't have too much money on you."

Gil accepted the money. "Would you like a root beer, Jan?"

"Sure."

Gil approached the A&W Root beer kiosque His heart raced. Standing behind the counter, was the man he had seen after Marie's murder and earlier that day at the North York Centre. A blond haired girl took his order.

When Gil returned to the table a few minutes later, he placed Jan's root beer in front of her. She thanked him. He shook Brandon's hand. "I realize this is difficult for you, but I'd like to ask you a few questions about April."

Brandon adjusted his glasses. "It's okay. The police have already talked to me. I never thought I'd be talking to them today. Why do you want to know though?"

"We want to find her killer?"

Brandon held up his hand. "Wait. You don't know what you're up against."

"I just want to find the killer."

Jan said, "April seemed distraught in the last e-mail she sent. She didn't like her time in Orillia."

Brandon said, "She told me she wanted to give up modeling. It wasn't what she had anticipated."

"Certainly not the drug involvement."

"She assured me she'd never stoop so low. She had no use for drugs."

"Me neither."

Gil sipped his root beer. "Brandon, Mrs. Ames, told us you'd had a problem with a photographer."

Brandon shook his head. "The guy was a real jerk. He kept hitting on April."

"What a creep!" exclaimed Jan.

"Do you know his name?" asked Gil.

Brandon wrinkled his forehead. "I believe it was Bob Taylor. Ever since she became a model, she's had problems with that guy."

"What does he look like?"

"About five ten. Husky build. Blond, curly hair. He's really cocky."

Jan sipped her root beer. "Did April mention Marsha Tulino?"

Brandon removed his glasses and sipped his pop. "She spoke the world of Marsha. Marsha was one of the few friendly people at the agency."

Jan lowered her head. She paused a moment, which was unusual for her. Finally she said, "Marsha's dead now too."

Brandon's jaw dropped. "You got to be kidding."

She shook her head. "I wish I was. Two murders in one morning are a bit much."

Gil patted her back. "We'll help put an end to all this."

Brandon buried his face in his hands. "I wish April would have listened to me. I told her not to go to Orillia."

Jan patted Brandon's hand. "Don't worry. It's not your fault."

"She had her doubts about going there."

At that moment Jan poked Gil. "Don't look now, but we got trouble."

Gil's heart raced. *What did Jan see? Was it the guys who had chased them?*

Chapter Six

Gil grabbed Jan's hand. "Let's get out of here."

Jan slapped Gil. "Don't be rude."

He breathed a sigh of relief when he heard Jan's sister Tiffany's distinct giggle. At fifteen she was a year younger than Gil and Jan. She was with Cindy Manuel, her best friend.

Tiffany rubbed Gil's shoulders. "Honey, you need to relax. You're tense."

The morning's events would make anyone tense, thought Gil.

Tiffany pressed her olive-complected cheek against Gil's. "I love you, honey." She was probably the biggest flirt Gil knew.

Jan grabbed her sister's arm. "Stop right now. I'm not in the mood for your garbage."

"Boy, aren't you crabby today. Get up on the wrong side..."

Cindy grabbed Tiffany's upper arm. "Chill, will ya. Gil and Jan have been crying."

She patted Jan's arm. "Sorry about that. What's the matter?"

Jan stared at the table. "Someone killed April."

Cindy's face turned pale. "Oh, my goodness. What happened?"

Jan related the story of the morning's happenings.

Cindy hugged Jan. "I'm sorry. She was so nice. I wish I could have seen her again."

Tiffany brushed away a tear. She also hugged her sister. "I'm sorry. I know you looked forward to seeing her. I liked her too."

Jan introduced her sister and Cindy to Brandon. Cindy grabbed Brandon's hand. "Wished I were meeting you under different circumstances."

Brandon could only nod. He wiped away more tears.

Tiffany patted his arm. "Sorry. She was so nice."

Nobody said anything for a few minutes. Gil finished his root beer and tossed it in a nearby garbage basket.

Tiffany said, "Maybe this isn't the best time to share this, but I got a modeling contract."

Jan's jaw dropped. "You're kidding me."

Tiffany shook her head. "No. April had told me to contact the agency."

Gil frowned. He had to warn her about the danger. "Tiff, I'm happy for you, but you may not know what you're getting into."

She patted Gil's hand. "Don't worry, honey. I can take care of myself."

Jan grabbed her sister's arms. "Tiff, listen to me. Two people are dead. That place is dangerous."

"I'll do what I want. After all, I'm beautiful."

"Suit yourself."

Gil frowned. Tiffany often insisted on getting her own way and later ended up in trouble because of it.

Jan asked, "Where are you going now, Tiff?"

"We'll walk around here for a while."

"Okay. See you later."

Gil held up his hand. "Wait. Have you talked to anyone at the agency?"

Tiffany brushed back her long, black hair. "Natalie Bergeron."

Brandon's face fell. "April had a problem with her."

"What kind?"

"Natalie kept offering her drugs."

Tiffany gasped, "Oh, no. I have an appointment with her this afternoon."

Jan said, "Tiff, I suggest you don't go."

"No, I'm going."

"Be careful."

"Please. You're not my mother."

Cindy wrapped her arm around Tiffany. "I'm going with her."

The two girls left.

Gil tensed. Just what would happen to Tiffany, he wondered. He prayed silently, "Lord, please surround Tiffany. Keep her from all harm."

Brandon checked his watch. "I better get going. I'm supposed to meet my cousin."

Gil held up his hand. "Wait. I'd like to ask you a few questions."

"Go ahead. Make them quick."

"When was the last time you saw April?"

"Tuesday night at my parents' house."

"What happened?"

"She told me she wanted to give up modeling."

"Why?"

"Because of her bad experience in Orillia."

"It was just you and she?"

"No, my sister and her boyfriend were also there."

"How were they to April?"

"Leah and April were close friends. In fact, Leah introduced me to her after a play they were both in."

Gil and Jan followed Brandon outside the Eaton Centre. Gunfire erupted. Gil pushed Jan out of the way of a bullet aimed in their direction.

Gil turned around and watched in horror as a guy around their age crumpled to the ground.

Chapter Seven

Gil grabbed his cell phone and immediately dialed 9-1-1.

Jan crawled toward the wounded youth. "Lord, don't let him die."

Brandon pulled a towel from his duffle bag and pressed it against the guy's bleeding lower abdomen. "Jeremy, hang in there."

Gil asked, "You know this kid?"

Brandon shook. "He's my cousin."

A crowd of people gathered around. Gil asked, "Did anyone see who fired the shots?"

Nobody, however, admitted to having seen who fired them. A few minutes later a number of police arrived.

Jan felt Jeremy's pulse. "Oh, no. It's getting weaker. Lord, don't let him die."

Gil breathed when the ambulance arrived. Two paramedics with a stretcher shouted," Let us through."

Brandon said, "I'm his cousin. Let me come with you."

Both Gil and Jan gave statements to the police.

An hour later Gil and Jan entered the waiting room of the emergency room at Sick Kids Hospital. Brandon sat there pale faced.

Jan patted his arm. "Any word on Jeremy?"

"He's stable."

Jan looked at the ground. "The bullet might have been meant for me."

Gil's body tensed. "We need to find the scum who did this. Nobody'll get away with hurting you."

After a brief pause Gil faced Brandon. "I realize this is a bad time for you, but please tell us more about the last time you saw April."

Brandon swallowed. "Like I said, it was at my parents' house. My sister greeted me at the door telling me April was there."

"Was this a surprise?"

"Yeah. I hadn't been expecting her. My sister assured me I'd like what I'd see. April was in her bikini."

Gil smiled approvingly. He turned his head so Jan wouldn't see his face. After all, she didn't like for him to look at other girls.

Brandon coughed. "My sister's boyfriend was there like I said. We had fun splashing each other in the pool. Then April told me we had to talk."

"You were probably thinking she wanted to dump you?"

Jan grabbed Gil's arm. "Honey, please. You're..."

Brandon raised his arm. "Jan, it's okay. I had thought that, but I couldn't understand why. I thought our relationship was going good. The problem was, however, with her career."

"What did she say?" asked Jan.

"Bob, the photographer, kept offering her pot. In fact, he lit one in front of her. She asked him to put it out. Plus she saw a couple of the models snorting cocaine."

Jan waved her arms. "That's crazy. No wonder she wanted to give it up."

After a brief pause, Jan placed her hand on Brandon's arm. "What a rotten thing to happen to your cousin. What's he like anyway?"

"He's from a small town near Guelph. He's home-schooled, but plays baseball for a Christian high school. He's never been in any real trouble."

"Poor kid."

"Maybe the two of you should go. Jeremy's parents are on the way. Thanks though."

Gil stood up. "Sure. We'll pray he pulls through."

Jan handed Brandon a piece of paper. "Here's my cell number. Please call us when you hear more about Jeremy. Also, if you can think of anything else concerning April."

Brandon accepted the piece of paper. "Will do."

Gil and Jan returned to the Eaton Centre to do some window-shopping. Gil's stomach growled. He hadn't eaten yet that day.

Jan glanced at him. "Are you all right?"

"Just famished. I hope I can eat now. What about you?"

"Yeah, I better eat something too. Mom always says it's not wise to not eat."

Mrs. Barrio was a nurse practioner and made sure her family ate right.

The two teens stopped at the north end food court. Gil pointed to A&W Root beer.

He really enjoyed their burgers.

Jan frowned. "No, I don't think I better."

Gil clutched her arm. "Don't worry. They have salads."

"Salad, it'll be then."

While Jan ordered a salad and bottled water, Gil ordered a chubby chicken with a root beer.

Gil munched on his sandwich. Events from the day raced through his mind. He figured there had to be a connection. But who? And why? He shared his thoughts with Jan.

Jan sipped her water. "I know what you mean. We don't even have a firm suspect."

Gil frowned. Jan grabbed his hand. "Honey, what's wrong? I mean besides what we've been through today."

Gil wiped his mouth with his napkin. "This haunts me."

"Why?"

"The disturbing similarity to Marie's murder."

"You mean that girl you knew in France."

"Exactly."

"What happened? Please tell me."

Gil told her about Marie.

Jan patted Gil's hand. "I'm sorry, honey. I wish I would have known." She finished her water. "Was the killer ever found?"

"No. That's what has motivated me to solve mysteries."

Jan pulled on her ear lobe. "So, you're saying this was similar to April's murder."

"Exactly. They were both blonds, Christians, and models."

At that moment Gil's cell phone rang. Who would be calling him? Few people had his number.

A male voice he didn't recognize said, "Tonight is the night you die."

Chapter Eight

Gil shivered. The caller ID had said, "Private Number." He didn't want to give in to the caller's threat. "Whoever you are, I'm not afraid of you."

The caller laughed. "That's what you think, punk."

Gil slammed his phone shut. Jan grabbed his arm. "You be careful. You may not know what you're messing with."

Jan tossed the remainder of her salad in the garbage. "So, what was Marie like?"

"Happy-go-lucky. A big tease."

Jan frowned. "Hmm…quite the opposite from April. Was Marie shot?"

"Yes."

Jan checked her watch. "I think we'd better get back to the hotel."

About ten minutes later Gil and Jan returned to the hotel where Mrs. Barrio and Jan's youngest sister Nadine sat on one of the beds.

Jan wrapped her arm around Nadine, who was a few inches shorter than her and had shoulder-length sandy brown hair. "How was your day, Munchkin?"

Munchkin was Nadine's nickname from childhood, as she always liked *The Wizard of Oz.* Nadine rubbed her chin.

"Good. We visited a few museums. The ROM was so cool."

Mrs. Barrio, who resembled Jan, brushed back her dyed blond hair. "You and Gil look like you've had a rough day."

Jan told her the day's events.

Mrs. Barrio wiped away tears. "I'm sorry. I loved April. She was such a sweet girl."

Nadine sobbed. "She was like another sister."

Jan hugged Nadine. "I felt the same way." She gently stroked her sister's hair. "I love you, Nadine."

Tears streamed down Nadine's soft, olive-complected cheeks. "Love you too, Jan. I hope you find whoever killed April."

Mrs. Barrio placed her hand on Jan's shoulder. "You kids be careful. I think you should stay out of it, and leave this to the police."

Gil slammed his fist on the bed. "No. We can't. We must find the killer."

Jan wrapped her arm around her mother. "Have you heard from Ramona?"

Mrs. Barrio shook her head. "I don't know how many messages I've left. She hasn't called me back."

"That's strange."

About two hours later Gil sat with the Barrios and Cindy at Tavanos, an Italian restaurant at the Eaton Centre. Their booth was near the bar where a television set played. Cindy, who hoped to one day go into broadcasting, took notes.

Jan glanced at the screen. "Oh, no."

Gil looked at the screen. The anchorwoman announced, "Metro Toronto Police are looking for the killer of Toronto model April Ames. Ames, 19, was shot to death outside the North York Centre library. Police are unsure of the motive as this time. Anyone with any information should call Metro Toronto Police at 324-2222."

The news clip showed a picture of April in a blue dress.

A minute later the anchorwoman continued," Later this morning police were called to the Bloor Street area underground shopping area where 28 year-old Marsha Tulino was found. Tulino was an agent of Francisco –Milano, a leading Toronto modeling agency. Police decline comment at this time as to whether there's a connection in the deaths."

Gil glanced at the picture of Marsha. She sure was beautiful, he thought. Why would someone want to kill her? He vowed to find out.

Jan ducked down. Gil grabbed her hand. "Is something wrong?"

"Don't look now. Those goons who were hitting on April and me are sitting at the bar."

A moment later the waitress took their orders. Mrs. B., who was a nurse practioner, made sure the group ordered plenty of garden salad. Gil and Jan both ordered lasagna.

His stomach growled. The meal from A&W Root beer hadn't stayed with him too long.

When the waitress returned with their drink orders, Gil asked," Those two men at the bar, do you know them?"

The waitress frowned. "Not personally. They are regular customers. Is something wrong?"

"They just look familiar." Gil didn't want her to know he suspected them of a crime.

A few minutes later the waitress brought the bowls of salad. After she left, Jan grabbed Gil's hand. "Don't look now, but Bartholomew's talking to those men."

Gil's heart raced. What connection did his English teacher have to these men? Was he involved in the murders of April and Marsha?

Mrs. Barrio frowned.

Jan asked, "Mom, is something wrong?"

"I still haven't been able to get a hold of Ramona."

"I know. You've called her many times."

"Right. She knew we were coming."

Nadine sipped her water. "Maybe she had to go out of town suddenly."

Mrs. B. stroked Nadine's soft brown hair. "That could be, honey."

The waitress returned to the table to refill drinks. She was probably around twenty years old. She was tall and slender and moved gracefully as though she'd been a dancer. Her nametag read Elaine.

Gil held up his finger. Elaine smiled at him. "May I get you something else?"

Gil shook his head. "But I'd like to ask you something."

"Sorry. I'm a bit old for you."

"Please. That's not what I'm asking. I was wondering if you knew April Ames."

Elaine frowned. "Why?"

Jan interjected, "She was a good friend of ours. She died this morning."

Elaine bowed her head. "I'm sorry to hear that." She bit the end of her pen. "I think I do know her. Didn't she work at Jean Machine for a while?"

"Yes."

"Now I remember."

"What?" Gil stuffed a forkful of salad in his mouth.

Elaine looked around the restaurant. "Maybe I can tell you later. I've got to get working."

Cindy nudged Gil. "You never stop, do you? You can't even enjoy a nice Italian meal without putting your nose into someone else's business."

Gil paused a moment to eat his salad. Finally he said, "Nope."

About ten minutes later, Elaine brought the entrées. Cindy had veal parmagiana with angel hair pasta, while the four other Barrios had chicken cacciatore with spaghetti.

Mr. B. prayed for the meal

Gil glanced over his shoulder. He quickly looked down and admired his entrée. Walking toward the table was Mr. Bartholomew."

The teacher stopped at the table. Gil continued to eat ignoring him.

Tiffany, however, waved to him. "Hello, Mr. Bartholomew."

The teacher patted her shoulder. "What's new with you, young lady?"

Tiffany flashed him a sweet smile. "I had an interview for a modeling job today."

Bartholomew frowned. "How can that be? You're American."

"A lady I met today told me to stop by the studio."

"Interesting."

Gil kept silent. He wished Tiffany hadn't told him, for he suspected Bartholomew was up to no good.

Bartholomew looked over Cindy's shoulder in an attempt to glance into her notebook. "What's a beautiful girl like you doing writing on your summer vacation?"

Cindy stuck her nose in the air. "I plan to either teach or have a career in media communications. As for you, mind your own business."

"What was that, young lady?"

"You heard me."

He seized her arm. "Watch your tongue."

"Let go of me, pervert."

"What was that?"

Cindy struggled to get loose from Bartholomew's grip. "You gave my sister a lower grade than you did to that tramp Sonja Harris. My sister's speech was way better."

Gil got up. He noticed some people looking toward their table. He didn't want this to develop into anything worse. .

"Excuse me, Mr. Bartholomew. Let Cindy go."

"Not until she apologizes."

Mr. Barrio approached the teacher. "She has no need to do so. Why don't you just leave?"

"Fine."

Bartholomew punched the table before leaving the restaurant.

Gil patted Cindy's arm. "Don't worry about him."

Gil turned toward Jan. Her face had grown pale. "Jan, what's wrong?"

Chapter Nine

"Somebody just sat at the table with those goons. He's the guy April couldn't stand."

Gil's face fell. His heart raced. "That's the guy I saw three years ago at Marie's murder."

Jan's eyes widened. "The pig gets around. He kept hitting on April every time he saw her."

Nobody said much during the rest of the meal.

Elaine stopped at the table. "Dessert anyone?"

Gil looked around the table. Some chocolate ice cream would be nice, he thought. Since Mr. Barrio was paying for the meal, however, he thought he'd better wait until someone else ordered.

Finally, Nadine broke the silence. "I'll just have some vanilla ice cream."

Everybody except Mrs. B. ordered ice cream. She rarely ate sweets.

Gil touched Elaine's arm. "One more question?"

"What now?"

"The guy who sat at the table over there. Do you know him?"

"Yeah. He works at A&W Root beer here in the mall. Please, I'm busy. Other questions have to wait."

Gil frowned. Perhaps Elaine knew more than she was letting on. Would he, however, have chances to ask her later?

A few minutes later Elaine brought the ice cream. She handed Gil a slip of paper. "Call me if you have any questions."

After Elaine left the table, Cindy winked at Gil. "Ooh…she likes you."

Jan kicked Gil underneath the table. "Don't get any ideas, buddy."

After dinner, Gil and Jan walked around the Eaton Centre.

Jan said, "I wonder what Bartholomew's really up to."

"I know what you mean. It's like he's trying to start something with us. Or worse.

Like setting us up…"

Jan's cell phone rang. Before she answered it, she glanced at the number. "How's he doing?"

A moment later Jan said, "We'll pray for him."

Gil held Jan's hand. "What's wrong?"

Jan squeezed his hand. "Jeremy's still in critical condition. Doesn't look good."

"Poor kid. I pray he pulls through." Gil pointed to the bench. "Let's pray right now. Lord, please help Jeremy to come out of this. Guide the surgeons and the doctors. Make him whole again. Amen."

Gil stood up. "Did Brandon say where he was at?"

"Still at Sick Kids Hospital."

"Let's go there."

Half an hour later Gil and Jan arrived at the hospital. The waiting room, however, was empty.

Jan frowned. "That's strange. He said he'd be here."

A nurse approached them. "Is something wrong?"

Gil grabbed Jan's arm. "Let's try the parking ramp."

The teens entered the parking ramp on the fourth floor. No sign of Brandon.

"Up or down?" asked Jan.

"Try down." Gil headed for the staircase.

"Wait!" Jan cried. "I hear something."

Gil listened too. He thought he heard Brandon's voice.

Another man said, "I'm going to mess you up, punk."

Gil and Jan ran up the stairs. When they got to the fifth floor, they saw Brandon wrestling with one of the men they'd seen at the restaurant. Gil hurried over to the man and shoved him into a car.

The man pointed at Gil. "What's the big idea, punk?"

Gil stood still. "Maybe you should tell me."

The man clenched his fist. "Who are you?"

Gil glanced at Brandon who looked like a defensive lineman ready to charge through an offensive line. "Name's Gil Leduc."

Brandon jabbed his finger toward the man's face. "Not finished with you yet, Taylor."

"As in Bob Taylor?" asked Gil.

"You know me, punk?"

"Let's say I've heard of you. What do you know about April Ames?"

Taylor sneered. "Think you're a cop or something?"

Jan stepped forward. "April was a good friend. We want to know if you know anything about her murder."

Taylor folded his arms. "Don't pin no murder rap on me."

"I'm not, but do you know anything?"

Taylor waved his hand. "I'll level with you. The other models hated her. Just another deeply religious, goody-two-shoes..."

Jan jabbed her finger toward Taylor's face. "She was a Christian who loved Jesus."

Taylor held up his hand. "I don't want to hear anymore." He pointed his finger at Gil. "Keep your nose out of my business if you know what's best for you."

Gil grabbed Jan's hand. "Let's go."

"You better."

Without further word Gil and Jan left the parking ramp. They decided to return to the hotel.

In the hotel lobby someone tapped Gil on the shoulder. He pivoted on one foot and faced Bartholomew.

Bartholomew smiled at him. "Funny we keep meeting like this."

"You're not following us, are you?" asked Gil.

The teacher laughed. "Not quite."

Gil said, "Sorry about our behavior earlier. We've been through a lot today."

Bartholomew pointed to a sofa in the lobby. "Let's sit down. I'd invite you to the bar to have a drink with me, but you're too young."

Gil didn't respond. Even if he were of drinking age, he wouldn't have accompanied the teacher into the bar.

Bartholomew rubbed his cheek. "Why was the day so rough?"

Gil informed him about April.

Jan added, "It was the girl you saw me with at Port Dalhousie."

Bartholomew said, "Yes. The model. She's dead, eh? Such a shame."

Jan hung her head. "Yes, it is. She was a good friend of mine. We were looking forward to having some fun with her."

"Listen. I'm sorry I bothered you at the restaurant."

Jan patted his hand. "It's okay. You'd have no way of knowing."

Gil, however, couldn't help but wonder if Bartholomew actually did know something about April's murder. He thought, however, he'd try a more subtle approach. "Who were the men you were talking to at Tavanos? "

The teacher shrugged. "Just a couple of blokes who wanted to chat."

Jan said," But you were at the table a while."

Gil added," The one's a photographer. His name is Robert Taylor."

Bartholomew jerked back in his seat. "Is there a problem?"

"Let's just say I believe they knew April."

Bartholomew checked his watch. "Sorry to have to end this chat so soon. I've got a phone call to make. Stop by my room later tonight. Maybe we can watch a movie together."

Jan said, "Sorry. We'll pass."

"Suit yourselves."

When the teacher was out of earshot, Jan asked, "What do you think?"

"He's got to be hiding something. He was stunned when I brought it up about the two men."

"I'll say." Jan brushed her hair away from her eye. "Go to his room to watch a movie. That'll be the day."

"I'd like to know who he's calling. Too bad we don't know his room number."

About five minutes later Gil and Jan joined the rest of the gang in the connecting rooms. Mr. Barrio shared the scripture, which said, "All things work together for good to those who love God."

He closed his Bible. "I know certain things haven't gone well for us today. We didn't expect April to die, nor for this Jeremy to get shot. We know April loved Jesus."

Jan wiped her eye. "Yes, she did."

Cindy hung her head. "She really lived what she believed. Too bad she's…"

Jan hugged Cindy. "We all miss her."

Mr. B. said, "Let's gather in a circle. I want to pray for Jeremy." After a pause, he prayed," Lord, you know how we've looked forward to this trip. We thank you for allowing us to get here safely. You know things have not gone as we hoped. Help us to keep our eyes on you. Heal Jeremy. Comfort him in this dark hour. We ask you for these things in Jesus' s name. Amen."

As soon as Mr. B. stopped praying, Jan's cell phone rang. She looked at the caller ID display. "It's Brandon. What's up?"

Jan put it on speakerphone.

Brandon said, "I'd like for you and Gil to come over to my apartment as soon as possible."

"What's wrong?"

"My apartment's been ransacked."

Chapter Ten

Gil's heart raced. Whoever was doing these things was sure relentless. "That's terrible. Where do you live, Brandon?"

"In an apartment at the end of Bogart Avenue. Get off the subway at the North York Centre station."

"We'll do."

After Jan clicked her phone shut, Mr. B. held up his hand. "Not so fast, guys. I'll drive you."

About half an hour later Gil, Jan, and Mr. B., greeted Brandon at the entrance of his apartment. Jan introduced him to her father.

Mr. B. extended is hand to Brandon. "Wish I were shaking your hand under different circumstances. Sorry about April. She was a wonderful girl."

Brandon wiped his nose with a Kleenex. He shook the extended hand. "Thank you. I...loved her."

A police officer entered the apartment. He introduced himself as Constable Clyde Alexander. Brandon introduced himself to the constable.

Gil looked around the living room. Whoever did this meant business, he thought.

Someone had torn the sofa cushions with a knife, broken the glass to the television set and a mirror, and written a threatening message in lipstick across a picture of April. It read: She's dead, you're next.

Gil's heart raced. If someone killed Brandon, would the person come after him or Jan? Whoever was behind this, had to be stopped."

Next Gil entered the kitchen. Someone had opened all the cupboards. Probably every dish Brandon owned lay broken on the floor.

Jan joined Gil in the kitchen. "How could anyone do this?"

Constable Alexander asked Brandon many questions. Gil hoped he could pick up a clue as to who could have done this.

Brandon said, "I received a threatening message today on my answering machine."

"I hope you saved it."

Brandon faced the constable. "I did."

A small group of people entered the apartment. Alexander explained they were from the crime lab.

"I'd like to hear the message as well," said Gil. He thought he or Jan might recognize the voice.

Alexander walked over to the phone with the young people. Brandon pushed the button to his answering machine. A female voice said, "Get out of town before it's too late."

A shiver went up Gil's spine. The voice sounded familiar. He was about to speak when Jan held up her hand. "Wait. Play it again."

Alexander pointed to Jan. "Someone you know?"

Jan wrinkled her forehead. "The voice sounded like someone from Jamaica. A friend of my mom who lives in town was born in Jamaica."

A minute later Brandon replayed the tape. Gil listened carefully as well. He had met the friend on a couple of occasions. Maybe he could figure it out. He, however, couldn't say if the voice belonged to Ramona Gonzales or not.

Alexander asked, "What do you think?"

Neither Gil nor Jan could give him a definite answer.

Jan asked, "Brandon, have you ever met Ramona Gonzales?"

Brandon frowned. "Don't think so. I've met the daughter."

"Where?" asked Alexander.

"At a party I attended with April."

Jan asked, "Did April talk to her?"

"She tried, but Naomi gave her the cold shoulder."

"Who's Naomi?" asked Alexander.

"Ramona's daughter," replied Jan.

Alexander wrote some notes. "Are you implying these women might have something to do with the murders or tonight's break-in?"

Jan said, "It's possible. I remember one time when Ramona visited us. Even though she tried to represent as many minority models as possible, she complained about the blond-haired models getting all the breaks."

Brandon said, "Naomi always tried to cut down April. She kept saying blonds were dumb. I know that's not true."

Alexander frowned. "Seems like we have people who didn't like your girlfriend, but what about you?"

Brandon folded his arms. "At the party I was mentioning, one of Naomi's friends offered me pot. I told her I wanted nothing to do with drugs."

"So, someone's trying to scare you off their trial."

"That's what it looks like, but who?"

Alexander asked, "April didn't live here with you, right?"

"No. I live here alone."

Gil said, "So, it was either a female who did this, or a guy using lipstick trying to frame someone."

Jan said, "Both possibilities could be true."

Gil rubbed his chin. "Question is what's true. I plan to find out."

Alexander frowned, but didn't respond to Gil's comment.

At that moment Brandon's phone rang. He lifted the receiver. Gil and Jan remained silent hoping to hear what the caller said. "Consider this your final warning. Leave Toronto or die!"

Chapter Eleven

Brandon's face turned pale. "Whoever you are, I'm not afraid of you."

The line went dead.

Jan patted his arm. "Are you all right?"

Brandon held his head between his hands. "Not sure."

Gil's heart raced. Even though the call was directed at Brandon, he felt the call was also directed at him. "Did you recognize the voice?"

"No."

Gil wrinkled his forehead. "Doesn't sound like Taylor. What about the guy who was hitting on you and April, Jan?"

"No. I don't recognize the voice either."

Gil held a finger in the air. "This afternoon Brandon you mentioned Natalie Bergeron. Did you have any problems with her?"

"I know she didn't like me."

Alexander asked, "Would this Natalie Bergeron have a reason to kill your girlfriend?"

"Possibly."

"Any specific reason?"

"I know they didn't like each other. Natalie offered April drugs."

Alexander frowned. “Is there someone you could stay with tonight, Mr. Batista?”

Mr. B. entered the room. “He may stay with us.”

Brandon said, “Thank you, sir. But I’ll stay with one of my friends.”

“You sure?”

“Yeah.”

About an hour later Gil and Jan joined the girls at the hotel swimming pool. Gil joined Jan at the shallow end. She nudged him. “Do you wanna race?”

Gil hesitated. Jan was on the high school’s girls’ swim team.

She poked him. “Come on. Don’t be chicken.”

Gil and Jan dove in the pool. In no time flat Jan had crossed to the deep end beating Gil.

At that moment Bartholomew entered the pool area. He smiled sweetly at the girls. Gil cringed. He couldn’t stand seeing an older man flirt with younger girls.

Bartholomew pinched Tiffany’s cheek. She wore a black one-piece bathing suit. “ What’s with the conservative swimsuit?”

Cindy touched the teacher’s arm. “You’re not supposed to notice that.”

Jan jabbed her finger toward Bartholomew’s face. “Lay off my sister.”

Bartholomew waved his arms. “Please. I was only asking a question.”

Jan said, "Cindy's right. You're not supposed to notice what a young girl wears. My sister's underage so beat it."

"You'll regret you said that come next school year."

Gil motioned Bartholomew to a bench. "I want to ask again. Did you know April Ames?"

"No. I just met her that day in Port Dalhousie."

"Where were you this morning around at 8:30?"

Bartholomew stood up. "I don't have to put up with this. Don't bother me again if you know what's best for you."

Gil's heart raced. He stood stunned not believing Bartholomew's threatening manner. He must have something to hide, thought Gil.

A thought occurred to Gil. Bartholomew had deep blue eyes just like April. *Could Bartholomew actually be April's long, lost father?*

An hour later Gil watched part of a baseball game on television with Mr. B. Gil hated baseball, but Mr. B., who had once pitched minor league baseball, loved the sport.

As Mr. B. sat in the easy chair, he yawned. He checked his watch. "Gotta up early for tomorrow's meeting. I better go to bed."

After reading a chapter out of the Book of John, Gil went to bed. He, however, tossed and turned for about two hours as he kept thinking about April's murder and some of the day's other events. He still felt the bullet, which hit Jeremy, was meant for either him or Jan.

Gil was jarred awake by the ringing of the phone. He propped himself up on one elbow and glanced at the glowing alarm o'clock. Who'd be calling him at 3:30 a.m.?

He answered the phone. A female voice he didn't recognize said, "Drop case or die."

Before Gil could say anything, the caller hung up. His heart pounded as he broke into a cold sweat.

Mr. B. opened his eyes. "What was that all about?"

Gil told him about the phone call.

"You didn't recognize the voice?"

Gil shook his head.

Just a moment later, Gil called the front desk. The night clerk answered.

"Did you transfer a call to my room?" asked Gil.

"Somebody asked to be transferred to your room."

"Male or female?"

"A male."

Gil bit his lower lip startled by the desk clerk's answer. "Anything you could tell me about the voice?"

"Yeah. It was a man probably around fifty."

"Did the call come from within or outside the hotel?"

"Outside."

"Thanks." Gil hung up. Was it Bartholomew who had called the hotel? If so, what woman was he in cahoots with? Gil intended to find out.

Around eight o'clock the next morning, Gil got up. Mr. Barrio had already left the hotel to attend a conference on terrorism at Police Headquarters.

After Gil showered and got dressed, someone knocked on the connecting door. He opened it. Before it stood Jan, who pointed to her watch. "Gil, this is late for you."

"Sorry." He explained about the late night phone call.

Jan's eyes widened. "Oh, my goodness. I wonder who's behind this?"

"Someone who doesn't want us to find April's killer."

Jan grabbed Gil's hand. "Let's have breakfast. I'm starved."

A few minutes later Gil sat across from Jan in the hotel restaurant. The waitress brought them hot chocolate and orange juice. After Gil sipped his hot chocolate, he grabbed Jan's hand. "Please give me a rundown of your weekend with April."

"Why?"

"It might give me a clue to the murders."

Jan shook her head. "I appreciate what you're trying to do. I'm not sure if…"

"Remember. Each detail's important."

"There you go."

That weekend Jan took the train from Niagara Falls, Ontario to Toronto. Mrs. Ames and April picked her up at Union Station. From there the trio headed to the Eaton Centre to shop and eat lunch.

"So far, nothing unusual."

"No."

Jan continued. That afternoon she and April sunbathed at April's house and listened to music.

In the evening they ate at a French restaurant on King Street and headed to a skating rink where girls from the modeling agency hung out. Her heart skipped a beat when she saw Mr. Bartholomew.

Gil commented, "That old guy sure gets around."

"He told me he knows people in the agency."

"I wonder who. Was he with anyone?"

"Not that I could tell. He was flirting with every girl in arm's reach. He was kissing a girl who was probably only thirteen."

"The man's sick."

"You're telling me. He was also commenting about her body."

"That's messed up. I wonder why Bartholomew kept showing up where April was. This has to be more than a coincidence."

"Or he was trying to use me to get to her."

"We have to find out."

Jan continued further. After they left the skating rink, Jan thought she and April were being followed by a black sports car.

Gil interjected, "Probably the one that chased us near April's house."

"You're probably right."

"Question is, who owns a car like that?"

After that Jan and April ran to the nearest subway station. They took it to April's neighborhood. When they got to April's house, April checked her e-mail. One was a threatening letter, which said, "Don't go to Orillia or die."

Gil placed his hand over his mouth. "You've got to be kidding me."

Jan lowered her head. "I wish I was. A nice girl like her shouldn't have gone through what she did."

"That's for sure."

Gil sipped his hot chocolate. "Did she call the police?"

A waitress took their orders. While Gil ordered a Belgian waffle and sausage, Jan ordered a cheese and mushroom omelet.

Jan brushed back her ponytail. "Yeah. The e-mail had come from either a chat room or a library."

"Did she know who might have done that?"

"She told me it could have been any of the models. Not too many of them liked her."

Gil wrinkled his forehead. "That's what we've been gathering. What we lack though is a motive other than that someone might have found out about her wanting to go to the police about the drug dealing."

"I know what you're saying."

Jan continued on with the weekend activities. That night April and she watched a movie together. They slept in until about ten before heading to the North York Centre

where April liked to have breakfast. At Café Balzac they drank coffee and ate French bread. Marsha Tulino joined them half an hour later.

Gil bit his lower lip. "Seems like someone knew April's routine. Someone knew where to find her yesterday."

Jan wiped away tears. "And ruin another chance of seeing a good friend."

Gil held her hand. Tears formed in his eyes as well. "I know what you mean. That's why we have to find her killer."

Marsha reminded April of her modeling shoot at Centre Island that afternoon. She let Jan accompany them.

That afternoon at Centre Island Taylor took numerous photos of April.

Jan jabbed her finger toward Gil's face. "That's when the pig and his friend hit on me. I would like to have slapped them.

Gil's body tensed. "What did he say?"

"First, he thought I was one of the models. Then he asked me if I'd join him for a drink. I told him I was underage."

At that moment Jan's cell phone rang. "Excuse me one moment."

The female caller said, "Drop case or die."

Chapter Twelve

Jan's olive-complected face grew pale. Gil threw his arms around her. "I can't believe this. That's the same person who called me during the night. "Do you recognize the voice?"

Jan shook her head. "Whoever she is, I wonder how she would have gotten my cell number."

"This is getting weirder by the moment."

"What do you want to do after breakfast?"

"I think we'd better talk to some people at the North York Centre."

Jan was about to speak, but she abruptly shut her mouth.

"Is something wrong?" asked Gil.

"Don't look now, but here comes trouble."

Tiffany and Cindy approached their table. Tiffany flashed Gil a flirtatious smile. "I love you."

Jan jabbed her finger toward her sister's face. "Stop right now. I'm not in the mood."

Tiffany straightened herself. "You won't talk to me like that once I become rich and famous."

"Keep dreaming, girl."

Cindy wrapped her arm around Gil. "I love you, honey."

Jan slapped her arm. "Watch it, chick."

"Boy, oh, boy. Aren't you crabby this morning."

Jan grabbed her arm. "Look. April was a good friend of mine. Can't you get it through your thick heads to leave me alone."

Cindy started to speak. Gil grabbed her arm. "Cindy, please."

Cindy stuck her nose in the air. "Well, since the two of you are being anti-social..."

Jan pointed to the door. "Get out now."

Gil wrapped his arm around Jan. "Please. Calm down. I know you're upset, but calm down."

"I'm sorry. That was the last straw."

About an hour later Gil and Jan entered Café Balzac. They ordered hot chocolate.

When the waitress brought their order, Gil showed her a picture of April. "Have you ever seen her before?"

The waitress looked at the picture. Tears formed in her eyes. "She was one of my best customers. I'm sorry..."

Jan patted her arm. "I'm sorry too. She was a good friend of mine."

The waitress wiped away her tears. "She often had breakfast here. Usually coffee and a grapefruit. Being a model, she didn't like baked goods too much."

"Did she come alone or with someone?" Gil hoped to learn more about April's routine.

"Sometimes she was alone. Other times she was with a woman whose name I believe was Marsha."

Jan hung her head. "She's dead now too."

"I saw it in the paper," said the waitress, who handed Gil a copy of the Toronto Sun.

Gil leafed through the newspaper. According to the article, April was shot to death outside the library in the North York Centre. A witness believes the shooter to be a tall woman. Suspect's face was hidden with a veil.

After the waitress left the table, Gil reported to Jan what he had just read. "Fat lot of good that tells us."

About fifteen minutes later Gil and Jan entered the library. A woman with long, brown hair and glasses whom Gil guessed to be about thirty approached them. "Need help with anything?"

Gil showed her April's picture. "Did you know her?"

The woman removed her glasses. "She looks familiar. I can't quite place her."

The youths followed her to the checkout counter. Gil showed the picture to a woman sitting there. That woman didn't know April either.

Before leaving the library, they asked a few more of the workers if they knew April. None of them claimed to know her.

As they left, Gil muttered, "Someone must be lying. Since April spent so much time here, you'd think someone would have known her."

"I know what you mean."

About minutes later, Gil and Jan stopped at Mrs. Ames's house. She invited them in. After they joined her in the living room, she wondered back and forth, her hands shaking.

Tears streamed down her cheeks.

Jan asked, "What's wrong, Mrs. Ames? Is something else bothering you?"

"Brandon was supposed to meet me this morning. He never showed."

Gil told her about Brandon's apartment.

Mrs. Ames exclaimed, "How awful! That poor kid's seen enough these last couple of days."

"I'd like to know who did this to him."

"You be careful, young man."

Gil rubbed his chin. "Has anything unusual taken place since Jan and I left yesterday?"

Mrs. Ames wiped away tears. "I got a disturbing phone call."

Jan placed her hand on Mrs. Ames's arm. "What happened?"

Mrs. Bates replied, "The caller said..."

The phone rang. Mrs. Bates put it on speakerphone before answering it. A female voice said, "April's dead. Brandon's next."

"Who are you?" shouted Jan.

The line, however, went dead.

A shiver went down Gil's spine. Why should a woman suffering from the death of her only child receive such a threat? Furthermore who would be so calloused to do so? Gil rubbed his forehead. "Did you recognize the voice?"

Mrs. Ames shook her head. "No, but it's the same person who called last night."

Gil said, "This shouldn't have happened to you." He paused a moment and glanced at Jan. "Don't you think it's the same person who called you this morning?"

"It's gotta be. But who?"

Mrs. Ames urged. "You kids be careful."

Jan adjusted her ponytail. "May we look at April's room?"

"Sure, but why?"

"We might find something."

"Okay."

Jan grabbed Gil's hand and led him to April's upstairs bedroom. He was wondering what she had in mind.

The room contained posters of the Beatles. Mrs. Ames had been a fan of theirs and passed on her love of their music to April. A big teddy bear sat on the bed leaning against the wall.

On April's desk, Gil noticed a picture of April standing on the *Island Princess,* the tour boat of Orillia. She wore a blue one-piece bathing suit. He studied the picture carefully. Jan nudged him. "Is something wrong?"

Gil grabbed another picture. This one showed April and a few other girls clad in bathing suits. On the solo picture, April smiled. On the other one, however, she frowned. "Jan, do you recognize any of the other girls?"

Jan carefully observed the picture. "Sure. One of them's Naomi Gonzales. She and April didn't get along."

Gil slapped his forehead. "I should have known it was her."

Jan patted his arm. "Don't worry about it. We've got to find Naomi. She might know something April's murder."

Gil pointed to the answering machine's blinking light. "Maybe we ought to have a listen."

Jan said, "But I don't..."

The ringing doorbell interrupted her thought. Gil raced down the stairs wondering who it could be.

When he got downstairs, he breathed a sigh of relief. Brandon stood at eh entrance his arms around Mrs. Ames. She led him to the living room.

As Jan descended the staircase, Mrs. Ames said, "Gil and Jan, if you would excuse us. Brandon and I have things to discuss."

Jan kissed Mrs. Ames. "Sure. Call me if we can help."

About five minutes later Gil and Jan stopped at the Gonzales house. They stood before the door hoping someone would answer. They wondered if Naomi might know who murdered April.

Since there was no answer, they decided to leave. As they were descending the front steps, Gil heard an old lady yell, "Who goes there?"

Chapter Thirteen

Gil froze in his tracks startled by the old lady. "Who are you?"

The old lady glared at them. "Second time in two days I've seen the two of you snooping around here. What's your business?"

Gil folded his arms. "Answer my question first."

"Don't speak to me like that, young man."

"Who are you?" Gil was losing his patience.

"Name's Mrs. Schmidt. Are you here to see Naomi?"

Jan replied, "Yes. We're her friends."

Gil bit his lower lip. He wasn't sure if Naomi was someone they could actually call a friend. He knew, however, he shouldn't reveal much information to the woman. "Would you know where we could find Naomi?"

"Probably at her jobs. She works at the Eaton Centre and at the modeling studio."

"Thanks." Gil started t walk away. The woman, however, stood in front of him.

"Excuse us."

"Who may I tell asked for her?"

Gil rubbed his chin pondering the question. He didn't want to give their names to the mysterious woman. "Just tell her friends from America."

Gil and Jan hurried away before the woman could say anything else.

About twenty minutes later the youths entered the Eaton Centre. A few minutes later they entered the Jean Machine where Naomi worked.

A blond-haired girl asked, "May I help you?"

Jan replied, "We're looking for Naomi."

The girl wrinkled her nose. "She's not here."

"Is she working today?"

"Was supposed to."

"What do you mean?" asked Gil. He hoped they could locate Naomi.

The girl replied, "She didn't show up for work. Didn't call either."

Jan gasped. "Oh, no. I hope she's okay."

The girl frowned. "Is something wrong?"

Gil looked at Jan. He wasn't sure if they should reveal the real reason for their visit. Jan nodded her head giving Gil the okay to state their business.

Gil ran his fingers through his hair. "You must have heard of the deaths..."

The girl's eyes widened. "You don't think she's dead, do you?"

Jan placed her hand on the girl's shoulder. "I sure hope not."

The girl asked, "You two are too young to be cops. Why are you asking about the murders?"

"April Ames was a good friend of mine. We want to find the killer."

"I wish I could help, but I can't. Good luck."

"Thanks." Gil was about to leave when Jan grabbed his arm.

Jan held up her finger. "Wait. Do you know where Naomi could be?"

The girl frowned. "Possibly at the modeling studio. Like I said, I really can't help."

Gil pointed at her. "How well do you Naomi?"

"Not very well. I only started working here last week."

"Sorry to bother you."

"Oh, no. Don't apologize."

Before leaving the mall, Gil and Jan looked in many stores hoping to find Naomi.

They thought she might be there somewhere. After an unfruitful search, Gil suggested they head to the studio.

About ten minutes later Gil and Jan entered the studio where the tall, brown-haired Natalie Bergeron greeted them. Gil studied her face. He believed he had seen her somewhere before. She spoke with a French accent.

Jan asked, "Have you seen Naomi Gonzales?"

Natalie shook her head. "Not in a while."

"Her mom?"

"Not her either. I guess she's hanging out with her boyfriend."

Gil raised his finger. "Would that be Peter Bartholomew?"

"I believe that's his name. Is something wrong?"

"Have you seen any Shiite Muslims around? I mean women with a veil over their face."

Natalie placed her hand on her chin. "Some live here in the city. I try to stay away from those people. I'm not a racist, but my cousin was killed by those people."

"When was this?"

"About three years ago."

"What was your cousin's name?"

"Why would you want to know?"

"Three years ago a girl who I liked died. She was found murdered at the train station in Tours, France."

Natalie gasped. "You've got to be kidding. What was her name?"

"Marie Chauvet."

"This is unreal. She was my cousin."

Gil stood there stunned. So someone dressed as a Shiite had also killed Marie. His uncle had declined to give him any information about the case.

Natalie motioned for the youths to sit down. "My cousin was a nice girl. I wished I had chosen the path she chose. I still cry when I think of her lying in that casket the purity ring on her finger."

Gil ran his fingers through his dark, curly hair. "How well did you know April?"

Natalie faced her desk. "I admit I was cruel to the girl. I thought not another good-goody religious type. I tried to push her into drugs. She wouldn't budge. Then I heard about her murder. Same m.o. as with my cousin..."

Natalie began to sob. "What a mess I've made of my life."

Jan padded her shoulder. "We'd like to help you."

Natalie crumbled up a piece of paper. "How can a couple of teeny boppers help me?"

"I know of people who can."

Gil asked, "How do you get along with Ramona?"

Natalie frowned. "Not too good. This is a competitive business, young man."

Jan stood up. "I think we'll let you go. We'll be in touch."

Gil and Jan headed toward the subway. Gil touched Jan's arm. "Where to now?"

"Centre Island. I know Naomi likes the beach there. I just wish we could have spent time there with April."

Gil wrapped his arm around Jan, who wiped away a tear. "I know what you mean. I was looking forward to it as well."

On the way toward Union Station, Gil frowned. He was thinking about the last two days' events. He and Jan still had no idea who killed April and Marsha or who shot Jeremy.

Jan grabbed Gil's hand. "Are you okay, buddy?"

"I just wish we could find the killer."

"I know what you mean. We still have no solid leads."

"Thank God we're still alive. But why are April and Marsha dead?"

Jan wrinkled her nose. "They must have been closer to something than we are. But someone doesn't want us to get too close to someone or something."

"But who and what?"

"I want to find out. Someone's also after Brandon."

"You mean someone besides Taylor?"

"Well, I don't believe he ransacked Brandon's apartment."

Jan leaned on Gil's shoulder. "I believe Naomi might know something."

"I hope we find her."

Around twenty minutes later Gil and Jan took the ferry to Centre Island. They headed toward the beach hoping to find Naomi. As they stood by a swing set, Gil heard someone yell, "Jan."

Gil looked around, but saw nobody he knew. Jan, however, nudged him. "Got someone who wants to talk to us."

Jan led Gil by the hand to a short, dark-haired girl who was drawing a picture of a boat on Lake Ontario. She introduced the girl as Christina Zakarian.

The bikini-clad girl extended her hand to Gil who shook it firmly. "I've heard so much about you, Gil."

Gil smiled. "Really?" He was unsure how to take the comment.

Christina said, "It was all good."

"That's good."

Jan held Christina's hand. "I'm sure you know about April."

"Yes. She was supposed to meet me here yesterday. She was a good friend."

Jan patted her arm. "We were hoping to spend time with her too."

Gil asked, "When was the last time you saw April?"

Christina hit her pen against her pad of paper. "Wednesday at my house. She had spent Tuesday evening with Brandon."

"Did she say anything in particular?"

"Told me she wanted to give up modeling. It was so unlike her to give up."

"That's for sure," said Jan.

Gil rubbed his chin as he focused on Christina's face. He knew she looked familiar. After a moment longer, he remembered seeing a picture with April that morning. "Christina, were you in Orillia recently with April?"

Chapter Fourteen

Christina's mouth dropped apparently caught off guard by the sudden change in the conversation. "Yeah. I was one of the models."

Gil asked, "Did you know of any drug activity within the group?"

"Yeah. I saw Taylor hand cocaine to one of the models."

"Did he offer you any?"

"Why do you want to know?"

"This may lead us to April's killer."

Christina dropped her pad on her beach towel. "I can't stand Taylor. He's a filthy pervert."

"What did he do or say?"

"April and I were relaxing in the hot tub together. We wore our bathing suits. He claimed we had too many clothes on."

"What a pig!" exclaimed Jan.

"That's not all. He wanted to take nude pictures of April behind the Aqua Theater."

"April never would have."

"Right. Plus it wasn't in the contract."

"Anything else happen?"

"April and I knew about a party Taylor was holding in his room. He tried to force us to join it. He even threatened to kill us."

Jan's eyes widened. "That's crazy. Then what did you do?"

"We had no other alternative, but to leave. We called the police. A woman officer took us to another hotel where we waited for Mrs. Ames to pick us up."

"Do you believe Taylor killed April?"

"No. He seems to be all talk and no action. Somebody offered to fight him, and he wouldn't.

"Can you describe that person?"

"It was an older man. I'd say in his fifties. Husky. Gray hair."

Gil gasped. "Oh, no. Sounds like Bartholomew. What were they arguing about?"

"It was over one of the girls."

Jan grabbed Christina's hand. "Have you seen Naomi?"

"Gonzales?"

"Yes."

"No. I haven't seen her since Orillia."

"She was there too?"

"Yes."

"Did she talk to April at all?"

"They spent quite a bit of time together at the beaches."

"You've got to be kidding."

"No. Naomi couldn't have been any nicer."

"That's something," said Gil.

Jan wrinkled her forehead. "That's odd. Mrs. Ames told us Naomi hated April."

Christina shook her head. "Not true. Naomi's mother hated April."

Gil picked up a handful of sand and dropped it. "Enough to kill her?"

Christina sipped water out of a bottle. "Wouldn't surprise me. Naomi's mother complained tall blondes got all the breaks. She felt April had stolen assignments from Naomi."

Jan looked around the beach. Although not many people were around, she lowered her voice. "You could be on someone's list."

Christina jerked back. "I never thought things would go this far. One more thing, Naomi's not speaking to her mom. She wants to give up modeling. She prefers retail."

Gil held Christina's hand. "You'd better come with us."

"Sure. I'll head to Oakville. I have a friend who lives there. In fact, she's trying to fix me up with a Christian modeling agency."

Gil and Jan waited for Christina to put on her t-shirt, shorts, and sneakers. Gil placed his hand on Christina's shoulder. "We stopped at Naomi's house and at Jean Machine. She was at neither place. Where do you think she could be?"

Christina shrugged her shoulders. "I don't know. Wish I could be of more help."

"You've already been."

"Thanks."

As the trio approached the dock to the ferryboat, Jan's cell phone rang. She glanced at the number. It wasn't one she recognized. She hit the speakerphone button. "Don't say I didn't warn you. This is your last..."

"Who are you?" shouted Gil.

The caller abruptly hung up.

Gil said, "We'd better contact Hilger."

Christina stood still. "Somebody doesn't want you guys to solve the murders."

"They won't scare us off."

"You guys are brave for doing this."

Jan dialed Hilger's cell phone. Unfortunately the best she could do was leave a message.

Gil and Jan walked with Christina to Union Station once the boat landed on the other side of Lake Ontario. She boarded a GO train to Oakville. Just before she boarded, Jan wrapped her arms around her. "Careful, honey."

"Hope to see you soon."

As Gil and Jan walked away from the train, Jan poked Gil. "Where to now, buddy?"

"Let's give the Eaton Centre another try."

About half an hour later, Gil and Jan arrived at the Eaton Centre where they looked for Naomi. Gil's stomach growled.

Jan asked, "Are you all right?"

"We'd better get something to eat."

About ten minutes later they entered the crowded north end food court. Gil's body tensed as he spotted Anno behind the A&W Root beer counter. Why would Anno have been at the scene of two murders? He had to find out.

Gil rubbed his chin as he pondered what he should order. A blond-haired teenaged girl asked for his order. He stood silent not quite knowing how he should approach the situation.

Jan nudged him. “Come on. We ain’t got all day.”

Gil ordered a chubby chicken sandwich and a root beer. Another teenaged girl waited on Jan.

Seeing Anno enter the kitchen, Gil lowered his voice. “Has your manager ever been to Tours, France?”

The girl said, “Yes. He loves it there. I believe he studied there.”

While Gil waited for his order, Anno passed the counter. Gil held up a finger. Anno’s glare caught Gil’s attention. Even though the manager was smiling, his piercing blue eyes seemed cold and calculating.

Anno faced Gil. “May I help you? I heard you asking if I’d ever been to France.”

“Right. That’s my birthplace. I thought I saw you there three years ago.”

“So, what’s the big deal? Small world, isn’t it?”

Gil asked, “Did you know April Ames?”

Anno shook his head. “Never heard of her.”

“I don’t believe you.”

“Whatever this is about, I don’t have time for.”

Gil grabbed Anno’s arm. “What about Marie Chauvet?”

“Never heard of her either.”

“Well, I say you’re a filthy liar.”

Jan received her order. She touched Gil’s elbow. “I’ll find us a table.”

Gil grabbed Anno's shirt collar. "Listen here. Three years ago I saw you at the train station in Tours, France. That's where Marie died. Yesterday morning I saw you at the North York Centre Library. That's where..."

Someone pressed a hand on Gil's shoulder. He turned and faced a security guard. "Is there a problem here?"

Gil related to the security guard what he had just said to Anno.

Jan approached them. "Hilger's on his way."

The security guard asked, "Who's that?"

"A Metro Toronto Police detective."

The security guard motioned to Anno. "You're coming with me."

About ten minutes later Hilger arrived at the north end food court. Gil related to him what had happened. Hilger pointed his finger in Anno's face. "I'm taking you to the station for questioning."

Gil and Jan continued to walk in the Eaton Centre. As they passed a clothing store, someone tapped Gil on the shoulder. His heart raced. Could it be the person who threatened to kill them?"

Chapter Fifteen

A tall, slender Afro-American teenager stood before them. Tears streamed down her pretty face. Jan embraced the girl. "Naomi, are you all right? We've been looking all over for you."

Naomi nodded. "Jan, it's been terrible."

Jan motioned to a free bench in the centre's hallway. "Let's sit down. Please tell me what's so terrible."

Gil handed Naomi a handkerchief.

She wiped away tears. "My mom kicked me out of the house."

Gil raised his eyebrows. "You got to be kidding? He knew of kids who'd been kicked out of their houses, but they were children of alcoholics who were abused. Naomi's mother was wealthy. He had thought their home life was good.

Naomi buried her face in her hands. "I wish I was. She acts now as if she can't stand me."

Jan hugged Naomi again. "Please explain. We want to help you."

Naomi wiped away tears. "I told her I wanted to quit modeling. She told me I was crazy. After all, I could go places April Ames couldn't. My mom claimed April stole jobs from me."

"Which I know she didn't."

"You're right. April wasn't like that."

Gil asked, "Does the name Steve Anno mean anything to you?"

Naomi glazed at the ceiling. "I think so. I believe he's someone my mom knows."

Gil glanced at the floor. He knew it probably wasn't a good time to be asking Naomi too many questions, but he felt he had to. "Do you know if your mom was ever in Tours, France?"

"I wish I knew. I know she's been to many places." She paused a moment. "Something else I wanted to tell you guys."

Gil and Jan both glanced at her. Gil wondered what she'd say now.

Naomi placed a hand on both Gil and Jan. "I became a Christian last week in Orillia."

Gil pointed toward the ceiling. "Praise God."

"That's great," said Jan.

Naomi stared at the ground. "I'm glad the two of you think so. My mom doesn't."

Jan patted Naomi's arm. "I'm sorry. I do know that's why the friendship between our moms is strained."

Naomi checked her watch. "Sorry. I must go. We'll need to talk later. Here's my cell phone number."

About ten minutes later Gil and Jan returned to the Holiday Inn. When they got to the rooms, Gil's body tensed. Sitting on the bed was Tiffany. A welt surrounded her right eye. He clutched her hand. "Tiff, who did this to you?"

Jan wrapped her arm around her sister. "Oh, my gosh! This is terrible. What happened?"

Cindy entered the room carrying a bucket of ice. She placed a bag of ice on Tiffany's eye. Tiffany squirmed. "That hurts."

Jan patted her sister's arm. "It's okay. We want to nail whoever hit you."

Tiffany winced in pain. "Today I had my appointment with the agency. Natalie Bergeron talked with me a while. She told me they wanted to take some pictures of me. I, of course, agreed. First, I modeled some fall fashions."

"What happened then?" asked Jan.

Gil patted Jan's shoulder. "Wait. I think we should call Hilger."

"Go ahead."

Gil dialed the number. He breathed a sigh of relief when the detective answered his cell phone.

"What's up now?" asked Hilger.

"If you could stop by the Holiday Inn on Carleton, we'd appreciate. We might have something for you."

"I'm on my way now."

About twenty minutes later Hilger entered the hotel room. "What do you got?" He quickly glanced around the room. He plopped down next to Tiffany. "Oh, my. What happened to you, young lady?"

Jan said, "Detective Hilger..."

"Call me, Adam."

"Adam, this is my sister Tiffany and her friend Cindy Manuel."

Hilger shook hands with the girls. "Back to my question, Tiffany."

"Taylor hit me."

"As in Robert Taylor?"

"I believe that's his first name."

Hilger held a small notebook and pen in his hand.

Tiffany told the detective about her experience at the modeling studio. Taylor had made lewd comments about her.

"How dare he!" shouted Gil.

"What a pig!" exclaimed Cindy.

Hilger waved his notebook. "Young people, please." He faced Tiffany. "I take it, you didn't like what he said."

Tiffany clenched her fist. "I felt like hitting him."

"Why did he hit you?"

"He wanted me to pose nude. I told him I was underage. I even showed him my purity ring." Tiffany let Hilger look at her hand. "Then he wrapped his arm around my throat and started swearing at me."

"Did you tell anyone at the studio?"

"No. I left as soon as I could."

Hilger touched Cindy's arm. "Were you with Tiffany?"

"Yes. Outside the door."

"What did you hear?"

"Taylor told Tiff she'd done a good job. Now it was time for her to pose nude."

Jan's cell phone rang. It was Naomi.

Naomi's voice shook. "I have diskettes from my mom's computer. She and Bartholomew are not only into drugs, but kiddy porn as well."

Gil gasped. "Oh, no. This is crazier than I thought."

Hilger nudged Jan. "Give me the phone. Your friend's name is Naomi?"

Jan handed him the phone. "That's right."

Hilger said, "Naomi, this is Detective Adam Hilger."

"Hi," she said.

"Listen carefully. I want you to hand those diskettes over to the police. I'll call my friend Erich Schmidt right now. He's with the Morality Squad. I'll arrange for him to meet you somewhere."

"Okay."

After Hilger hung up with Naomi, he focused on the group. "Should any of you see Taylor, Bartholomew, or Mrs. Gonzales, call the police immediately."

Gil tapped Hilger on the shoulder. "What about Steve Anno?"

"He's cooperating. He still denies knowing who the murderer is. I've proven though he studied in Tours, France. He did admit to having been involved in the local drug trade.

"Okay," said Gil, who knew he had to find Taylor soon. The question was though, was Taylor the killer?

Chapter Sixteen

Around eight o'clock that evening Gil and Jan accompanied Tiffany, Cindy, and Naomi to a roller skating rink. Out of the corner of his eye, Gil saw Taylor entering the men's room. Not wanting to cause any alarm, he mentioned nothing to Jan.

While Gil and Jan skated hand-in-hand around the rink, he noticed numerous teens entering the men's room. Taylor hadn't come out.

Jan asked, "Is something wrong?"

Gil replied, "I'm headed to the men's room. Call Hilger."

He skated away before Jan could ask him anything.

Gil entered the restroom and washed his hands trying to not get too easily noticed. In the stall he could hear money being exchanged. More than likely, Gil thought, Taylor was dealing drugs to the kids.

Gil was about to leave, when he heard Taylor shout, "Not so fast, kid."

He twirled to face the photographer. "Suppose you tell me why you killed April Ames."

"I didn't."

Gil's body tensed. "Who did?"

Taylor laughed. "I don't know."

"You're a liar, Taylor."

Taylor clenched his fists. "Put them up. I'll do to you what I did to that sluttish friend of yours."

Gil quickly removed his skates knowing he couldn't fight on them. He whipped them against the wall. "I'll ask you again. Why did you kill April Ames?"

Taylor swung at Gil. "I didn't kill the little whore."

Gil blocked the punch. "She wasn't a whore."

Gil swung connecting with Taylor's abdomen. Taylor keeled over. Gil then kicked Taylor in the face causing the photographer to land flat on his back. Seeing Taylor reach in his pocket, Gil pounced on him.

Taylor, who outweighed Gil, tried to pin him to the ground. Gil fought back, however, with all his might. At one point, he pounded Taylor in the nose causing the photographer's nose to bleed.

At that moment someone kicked the door in. Hilger and a pair of uniformed constables stood over them with their service revolvers drawn. Hilger inched toward them. "Both of you freeze."

Hilger motioned Gil aside as he inched toward the photographer. He seized the photographer's neck. "What do you have to say for yourself, Taylor?"

Taylor spat at Hilger. "Nothing, pig."

Hilger glanced at Gil, who took it as a sign to leave the washroom. More police officers entered the rink. They had arrested a few of the kids.

The girls approached Gil. Jan patted his arm. "Are you all right?"

Gil wiped the blood off his hand from Taylor's nose. He told her about the fight.

Jan frowned. "If he's not the murderer, then who is?"

Gil wrapped his arm around her. "Let's discuss this later."

Two uniformed officers led a handcuffed Taylor out of the restroom. Hilger approached the teens. "Meet me at Police Headquarters. I need statements from you."

About half an hour later Hilger pointed at Gil. "I don't know whether to tell you you're brave or very stupid. Sure, you helped us put a dangerous criminal behind bars, but you could have been killed."

Gil nodded, not knowing quite how to respond.

Hilger tapped his pen on the desk. "We have enough evidence to put him away for years."

Gil rubbed his chin. "He claims he didn't kill April."

Hilger stretched his arms "That could be. I'm not convinced he's the killer either."

Jan asked, "Why?"

Hilger replied, "I've arrested a number of photographers in my twelve years on the force. I don't think Taylor would have shot April at the North York Center. Had he wanted to kill her, he might have already done so in Orillia."

Jan frowned. "Why?"

"Less chance of getting caught. I doubt he knows too many people there."

Gil said, "So, you're saying photographers usually kill models when they're alone with them?"

"Exactly. Plus, whoever shot April, Marsha, and Jeremy can probably move quickly. Taylor..."

"Is a little flat-footed."

"You're on the ball, kid."

Jan brushed back her hair. "That would also leave Bartholomew out for sure. Earlier I'd said we didn't suspect him anyway."

Gil ran his fingers through Jan's hair. "If he'd been the shooter, we'd have found him somewhere dead of a heart attack."

The two teens looked at each other without saying a word. Gil said, "I think I have this narrowed down. I just need proof."

Hilger waved at them. "Remember, I'm the detective. Be careful out there."

Tiffany, Cindy, and Naomi also gave statements to Hilger. Gil and Jan waited in the hallway for them. He knew it wouldn't be wise to let the three girls walk alone in downtown Toronto.

About an hour later the teens returned to the hotel. Gil and Jan hoped to talk a while at Second Cup in the hotel. Just as they were about to enter the hotel, a car sped down Carleton Street. Down the street from the hotel, the car made a U-turn. Gil yelled, "Quick. Inside."

The teens had just entered the hotel when a gunshot hit the door. Gil and the other teens remained close to the ground. He grabbed his cell phone and promptly dialed 9-1-1.

Chapter Seventeen

A crowd of people gathered around them. A man in his thirties identified himself as the manager on duty. "Are you kids, okay?"

The teens slowly stood up. The manager pointed to the door. "Why don't you come in my office?"

The teens followed him. Gil and Jan sat in the chairs in front of the manager's desk. The others sat on the floor.

He asked, "Are you guests of the hotel?"

"Yes," replied Gil.

"Have you had problems during your stay here?"

Gil looked at him not sure how much information he should reveal to the manager. "Yes."

"As in?"

"A prank call."

At that moment someone knocked. The manager answered. Before the door stood a police constable. "What have we got here?"

Gil stood up. "Someone's out to kill us."

"Who?"

"Don't know. Someone fired a shot at us."

Gil gave him a rundown of some of the other things that had happened during their stay in Toronto.

The constable said, "You kids be careful. Call us if you need anything."

The teens left the office. Jan grabbed Gil's hand. "I think we need a swim."

Gil wrapped his arm around her. "I agree."

About twenty minutes later Gil and Jan sat in the Jacuzzi by the hotel swimming pool. Gil gazed at the ceiling. Jan poked him. "What's on your mind, buddy?"

Gil replied, "I just wish we had something more concrete to go on. I know both Natalie Bergeron and Ramona didn't like April."

"Right."

"Was either of them in Tours three years ago? That's what we don't know."

Jan wrinkled her forehead. "Wait. Now I remember. Naomi told me her mom would be in Paris, France. She had also planned to go to the Loire Valley. She remembered reading about that area in a French class."

Naomi, who'd been swimming in the pool with Tiffany, Nadine, and Cindy, joined Gil and Jan in the Jacuzzi. "Did I hear my name mentioned?"

Jan wrapped her arm Naomi who wore a black and white patterned one-piece bathing suit. "I was just saying, I remembered your mom having been in France three years ago."

"Yeah?"

Gil said, "I was there too at the time. A girl I liked there was murdered."

"Wait. Are you suggesting my mom's a murder?"

"Can you tell me where she was at 8:30 yesterday morning?"

Naomi's jaw dropped. "You really do believe she is."

"Can you answer my question?"

"I know she'd already left for work."

Jan said, "Plus your mom knew about our plans to come here."

Naomi sat stunned unable to talk. "I cannot believe it. My own mother…a murderer. She used to take me to Sunday school. That changed, however, shortly after my parents' divorce."

At that moment Nadine, who wore a purple tankini, stepped in the Jacuzzi. "May I join you guys?"

Jan smiled. "Sure, munchkin."

Naomi stroked Nadine's soft brown hair. "Wish I had a little sister. Especially one as sweet and innocent as you." Naomi wrapped her arm around Jan's youngest sister. "Don't do what I did. I slept with my boyfriend and ended up with STD. "

Jan placed her hand on Naomi's arm. "That's terrible."

"Tell me about it. I found out at a clinic in Orillia. Except for April and Christine, the other girls deserted me. Treated me like a leper."

Nadine hugged Naomi. "I'm sorry."

Jan asked, "Nadine, tell me something. Was Mom ever able to get a hold of Ramona?"

"No. I don't know how many times she tried."

Naomi said, "I just couldn't understand her. My mother, I mean. I wished she never would have met that sleaze ball Bartholomew."

"Where did they meet?" asked Gil.

"Before a Shakespearean play in Stratford."

Gil jumped in the swimming pool and swam toward Tiffany and Cindy. They both splashed him when he approached him. He placed his hand on Cindy's shoulder. "I want to ask you something."

"Sure, lover boy."

"What has Lizzie ever said about Bartholomew?"

Lizzie was Cindy's older sister and a close friend of Jan. She was the editor of their high school's newspaper. Bartholomew directed their high school's plays.

Cindy frowned. "He often travels here to Toronto and Stratford. He appeared in many plays. "

"Tell me something. Do you think Bartholomew could be April's father?"

Cindy placed her hand on her chin. "Come to think of it. When I first met her, I looked her in the eye. Her eyes looked familiar. Later I had the same thought. She said her father left her when she was little."

"Anything else?"

"Wait. Yeah. He once played the disciple Bartholomew in *Jesus Christ Superstar.*"

"That's how he took the name."

That night Gil lay awake in bed. He just couldn't get the last two day's events out of his mind. If Ramona wasn't the killer, who was?

Not wanting to wake-up Mr. Barrio, Gil took his laptop and headed to the hotel lobby.

He plugged it in and wrote e-mail to his uncle. He was hoping he'd be able to help him find something out about Natalie Bergeron.

After Gil sent the letter, he realized something else. Sure, he and Jan focused more on trying to figure out who killed April. What hadn't occurred to him though was had there been a conflict between Natalie and Marsha? Perhaps he could find out from Naomi.

Gil returned to his room. He tossed and turned most of the night, his mind still on the case. Finally, he fell asleep.

He was jarred awake by the banging on the adjoining door.

Chapter Eighteen

Gil jumped out of bed. Before the door stood Jan. He touched her arm. "What's wrong?"

She shouted, "Naomi's gone."

Mr. Barrio got up. He wrapped his arms around her. "Why don't you have a seat."

Jan sat on the floor. "Where would a girl go at five in the morning?"

Gil put on a pair of jeans and a black t-shirt. "I'm going to the front desk. Maybe somebody saw her."

A few minutes later Gil approached the front desk.

The clerk asked, "May I help you?"

Gil described Naomi. "Have you..."

"Yes. She left here a few minutes ago."

"Did you talk to her?"

"She asked for a cab to Union Station."

"How much does a cab there cost?"

"Roughly twenty bucks."

"Thanks."

Gil checked his wallet. He had plenty of money for the cab ride. He checked outside and noticed a cab sitting in front of the hotel.

The cab driver asked, "Where to?"

"Union Station."

About ten minutes later Gil arrived at Union Station. Hardly anybody was walking around at that time.

Gil entered the huge trains station, which brought back memories of his times in France and Germany. Unfortunately it was also in a train station where Marie died.

Only a few people were on the main level. The ticket window and the doughnut shop were open. Naomi probably wouldn't be at the doughnut shop, he reasoned. After all, she was a model and was careful about what she ate.

Gil approached the ticket window. He described Naomi to her hoping she could tell him something.

"I can't give out that information, son," she said.

"Mam, this concerns a murder investigation. This girl's life may…"

"Please. You're much too young to be a cop. Just…"

At that moment Gil heard a young woman shouting. He quickly ran to the lower level heading to the departure area. His heart raced when he saw Naomi shouting at someone dressed like a Shiite Muslim and Bartholomew.

Gil called the hotel asking for Jan's room. Cindy answered the phone.

"It's Gil. Is Jan there?"

"Gil, honey. We've been looking all over for you. Where are you?"

"I'm…"

Jan then came to the phone. "Yeah. Where are you, buddy?"

"Union Station. Naomi's arguing with her mother. Call Hilger."

"I will. Wait for me there. My dad and I'll take the subway."

"Okay. Bye."

Gil inched closer to Naomi. He held his finger to his lips indicating to Naomi that she shouldn't say anything to him.

Naomi shouted, "I'm sick of you, Mom. I want to choose my own friends. I don't want to be a model."

"Suit yourself," shouted Ramona.

Naomi slapped Bartholomew across the face. "I hate you! You're nothing but a sick pervert. I hope you spend the rest of your life in jail."

Gil called the police and requested officers to come immediately to Union Station.

Bartholomew reached in his suit coat pocket. Fearing the teacher might have a gun, Gil lunged at him. The teacher, however, threw Gil off his back. He twirled to face the youth.

Gil stood up and dodged a karate kick from Ramona. Naomi charged at her mother and wrapped her arm around her mother's neck. Her mother, however, flung her over her shoulder. Gil threw a punch connecting with the teacher's soft abdomen.

The teacher, however, drew a gun. "This'll be the end of you, super sleuth. You just never learn, do you?"

Gil prayed a silent prayer. Ramona pulled a pistol out of her purse and pointed it at Naomi. "Nobody moves."

Bartholomew motioned to Gil. "Get moving, Frank Hardy. You're taking a ride with me."

Gil walked in front of Bartholomew who held the revolver at his back. He heard sirens approaching. "You won't get away with this, Bartholomew. Just like your lady friend won't get away with the murders of Marie Chauvet, Marsha Tulino, and April Ames, aka, your daughter."

Gil faced the teacher. Bartholomew snarled, "You're clever, Leduc. You, however, won't get out of this one alive."

"Why'd you do it?" shouted Gil. "You destroyed the lives of three wonderful girls."

More people were now in the train station. Many stood in horror. Three Metro Toronto Police officers stood by the Front Street exit with their guns drawn.

Bartholomew shouted, "Back off or the boy dies."

At that moment Mr. Barrio shouted, "Drop the gun, Bartholomew. You don't have a chance."

Mr. Barrio crouched behind a garbage can with his service revolver drawn. Hilger and a couple other Metro Toronto Police constables stood with their service revolvers drawn.

Gil prayed silently. He knew he had to act now. Bartholomew probably wouldn't pull the trigger being surrounded by so many officers. Gil stepped on the teacher's foot.

Bartholomew shrieked in pain. Gil fell down. The teacher pointed the gun at Gil. "I'll kill you."

"Drop the gun!" ordered a constable as the approached the teacher.

Bartholomew's hands trembled. Gil believed the teacher had never even fired one in his life. Gil got up and kicked the gun from Bartholomew's hand.

Naomi dove at her mother's feet as her mother fired a shot at the officers. Ramona fell backwards-losing control of the weapon.

The police raced in quickly pushing Bartholomew to the ground and slapping handcuffs on him. Hilger and a constable approached Ramona. The constable cuffed her.

Bartholomew stared at Mr. Barrio. "You're out of your jurisdiction, pig."

"Guess again. I'm taking you to the States. We've got enough evidence to bury you."

Naomi sobbed as the police led her mother away. Gil wrapped his arm around her. "I'm sorry."

"I wish she would have listened to me. I never wanted to hate April."

"What are you going to do now?"

"Call a lady from my church."

Gil held out his hand. "Keep in touch."

She shook his hand. "I will."

Around two o'clock that afternoon Gil sat on the beach with Jan in Port Dalhousie. He wrapped his arm around Jan.

Jan rubbed his back. "What's on your mind, Gil?"

Gil said, "Just reflecting on this case. I never would have thought Ramona would have been so spiteful. I mean to kill three people."

"I know. Dad said she made a full confession at Police Headquarters. She was motivated by hatred for blonds. I guess that's why I became a target."

Gil kissed her cheek. "Well, thankfully she missed."

Gil paused a moment. "Now I can put something else to rest."

"What's that?"

"Marie's murder. Three years I waited to catch her killer."

"I think you should take it easy for now."

Gil rubbed his chin. "Mmm…I'll have to see about that."

Jan said, "My mom would like for you to join us again next month when we go to Orillia."

Tiffany and Cindy approached Gil. Tiffany had announced earlier that morning she would no longer pursue modeling. Jan and Cindy had convinced her talent and personality would be better used elsewhere. Cindy flashed Gil a flirtatious smile. "So, lover boy, wanna take the nickel-a-ride?"

Gil frowned. He hadn't been on a merry-go-round in a few years. Cindy was referring to the beach's 100 year-old carousel. "I think I'll pass."

Cindy poked him "Are you too cheap to spend a nickel?"

Gil stood up. "That does it. I'm coming with."

Jan jabbed her finger toward Cindy's face. "You just watch it, honey."

Cindy's eyes brightened. "Don't worry. I'll make sure he won't get involved in another mystery."

Gil followed the girls to the carousel. He couldn't quite describe it, but he sensed another mystery would soon be in the air.

About the Author

Jim Toner's eclectic life includes a Bachelor's Degree in French from Houghton College and a Bachelor's Degree in Accounting from Niagara University. He has worked for the last eleven years as a youth sponsor at his church. He has completed three courses of the Institute of Children's Literature.

Over the years he has edited a few church newsletters and was briefly the leader of a writers' group in Southern Ontario. He's a member of the Word Guild. He has written for the Rock Express Management Newsletter and has seen his softball articles published in The Niagara Gazette. He has had a few letters published in Le Journal Français.

Currently he works for a Buffalo area accounting firm.

His interests include reading, writing, foreign languages, bicycling, softball, football, basketball, and hockey. He's a loyal fan of the Niagara University Purple Eagles ladies' basketball team.

His varied travels include Germany, France, Belgium, Holland, the three West Coast states, and various parts of Canada. He has taken the nickel-a-ride in Port Dalhousie.

The Purity Ring Murders is the second novel in the Gil Leduc series. Under the Blood was his first novel.

Printed in the United States
60332LVS00004B/4-6

9 781425 928421